The Mine of Lost Days

The Mine of Lost Days

Marc Brandel

Illustrations by John Verling

J. B. Lippincott Company · Philadelphia and New York

U.S. Library of Congress Cataloging in Publication Data

Brandel, Marc, birth date
  The mine of lost days.

  SUMMARY: On a visit to Ireland, Henry falls into a "haunted" copper mine, and discovers that he and his new friends can travel into the
past.
  [1. Space   and   time—Fiction.   2. Ireland—Fiction]   I. Verling,
John, illus.   II. Title.
PZ7. B7362Mi   [Fic]   74-8051
ISBN-0-397-31587-2

For TARA

The Mine of Lost Days

One

IT was Henry's mother who took him to New York to see him off. She wasn't allowed to go all the way to the plane with him. Henry had to be handed over like a package to an airline hostess at John F. Kennedy Airport.

"You bring him to Gate Four in twenty minutes," the hostess said. "I'll be waiting there for him."

Henry was left alone with his mother in the huge, crowded hall. She kept squeezing his shoulder and clutching his hand without saying anything.

A lot of things that Henry was used to, things he had never thought about before, had been changing lately.

He couldn't understand it.

The changes had started at the beginning of winter, about the time the first snow fell in the Hudson Valley. His mother and father started talking to each other like two people who had just met in a supermarket. He could hear them downstairs when he was in bed at night. Their voices were strained and different. His mother took to going to New York with a lot of other women and didn't come back until Henry was in school the next day. He would find her angrily making his bed when he got home in the afternoons.

Now Henry's father had driven off to a place called Black Mountain. He was going to teach there all summer. His mother was going to work in New York. Henry was being sent to Ireland. Everything was changing.

He didn't try to understand it much. He felt lazy in school. He would sit at his desk and not listen to what the teacher said. His father read his report cards and was puzzled and worried. He asked Henry what the matter was.

At the airport Henry's mother was clutching his hand so hard she hurt his fingers. When he asked *her* what the matter was, she bought him a candy bar. He put it in his pocket. His mother peeked at her watch again and took him to Gate Four.

The hostess was waiting for them. Henry's mother kissed him several times. She did it as though she didn't have time to do it properly. One of her kisses caught him in the eye. When she let go of him he followed the hostess down a long passage. He made up his mind he wouldn't look back when he got to the end of it.

He did, though, and his mother was still standing where he had left her.

She didn't move when Henry looked back.

Two

THE hostess was thin and friendly. Once the plane was flying over the clouds she kept stopping by Henry's seat and asking him questions about himself.

"How old are you, Henry?" "Where do you go to school?" "Do you like Ireland?" She listened to his answers too.

Henry told her he had never been to Ireland before.

"What are you going to do there?"

"Stay with my aunt."

"Does she live there all the time?"

Henry didn't know much about his aunt. She was his mother's older sister. Her name was Penelope Fallon. When his mother decided to get a job in New York she wrote to Penelope and asked her if she could have Henry for the summer. After a long time the answer arrived covered with small stamps with animals on them. The letter was opened at breakfast. Henry's mother read some of it aloud.

"I don't mind Henry coming to stay here if he's under sixteen. I find I don't understand adults any more, even when they're grown up."

There was a lot of talk about Penelope's letter after dinner that evening. Henry was sitting on the porch reading a book about Indians. He had begun to think more and more about Indians lately. He wished he was a Cheyenne. He could hear those strange sharp voices in the living room.

Henry's father didn't seem to like Penelope.

"Do you want to take him to Black Mountain with you?" Henry's mother asked at last.

Henry's father never answered that question.

Henry didn't tell the air hostess this. He said his father had given him a book called *Tom Sawyer* and he was going to read it every day. The hostess brought him more dinner than he could eat and he fell asleep. When he woke up most of the lights were out, a baby was crying, and his neck hurt. He kept telling himself all he had to do was just sit there. The journey would have to come to an end sometime.

It did. At last. Henry had to wait until everyone else had left the plane before he followed the hostess down the steps. The wind blew his hair into his eyes.

"Will Mr. Henry Travers please come to the information desk. Henry Travers."

Hearing his own name over the loudspeaker was like wearing a new suit for the first time. Henry thought everyone was looking at him. It made him feel shy and important.

Two girls in green uniforms were whispering to each other behind the information desk. A big woman with short hair was standing in front of it.

"So you're Henry." She was looking at him. "I'm glad you're so young. It'll be easier to talk to you."

The hostess squeezed his shoulder. "Have a good summer now."

Henry said, "Thanks." He watched the hostess walk away. Her skirt was higher on one side than on the other.

He was alone with his aunt.

She looked like one of the men who came to empty the garbage cans at home every Wednesday. She was wearing the same kind of coveralls with a sweater underneath. He wasn't sure it was going to be so easy to talk to *her*.

There was a little blue car in the parking lot outside. Aunt Penelope threw Henry's suitcase into the back as easily as the men tossed the cans up to be emptied.

They drove through a small city in which everything looked old. After that Aunt Penelope stopped the car several times and told him to look at the scenery. There were lakes and valleys and mountains as big as the Catskills but without any trees on them. Henry looked at them when he was told to. He found the candy bar in his pocket and ate it. They were still in the mountains when he fell asleep.

"Almost there."

The car was bumping along a narrow road. It was just dirt and stones. They seesawed up and down over a bump. Aunt Penelope stopped the car again.

"That's Roaring Water Bay."

Henry looked at the sea with the islands in it. Roaring Water Bay was very calm. He liked the islands. You could explore an island better than any other kind of place if it wasn't too big. Near his side of the car was a row of stone houses without any roofs on them. On the other side was a tall chimney. Henry had seen chimneys like that in Connecticut, but they had all been on top of old factory buildings. This one stood up straight out of the ground. He asked what it was for.

"That's the old copper mine."

Henry decided his aunt hadn't heard him. It

wasn't a mine. It was a chimney, a smokestack. There must be something below it, at least a fireplace. As he looked, he saw a tiny trail of smoke drift away from the top of it.

"Is there someone down there under the ground making a fire?" he asked.

His aunt didn't seem to hear that either. "I had to buy this whole hill," she said. "They were going to tear down those cottages and build villas for retired English people." She started the car. "The local people don't come here much. They say they've seen smoke coming out of that chimney and they think the place is haunted."

The car bumped down the hill, over some deep ruts, and stopped at a gate.

"The idiots think there are ghosts in the copper mine."

Three

FOR a long time Henry hated being in Ireland.

It wasn't so long really, only two weeks, but when you hate anything a day seems endless.

Penelope—she told him so often not to call her Aunt that he made himself think of her as Penelope— Penelope was friendly enough. He didn't see her much. She spent most of her time in a big stone barn near the house, chipping away with a hammer and chisel. She was a sculptor. She took Henry out to see her sculptures the first morning he was there. They were huge lumps of stone with little bits hacked off them and smooth places where the bits had been.

Henry pretended to be interested in one of them. "That's not finished."

It was hard to tell which ones were finished and which ones weren't.

After that Henry only saw Penelope at breakfast and hours later at dinner. She didn't talk at breakfast. She talked at dinner but it was no good answering her. Even when she asked him a question she went on talking without listening to what he said. Henry thought that perhaps after chipping away at those stones all day, "Chink." "Chink." "Chink," she couldn't hear anything when she stopped.

Another thing that made him think this was true was that she never answered the telephone. It rang several times every day. Henry could hear it ringing out in the barn too. Penelope never paid any attention to it.

She never paid any attention to letters either. The postman came every morning and pushed them under the door. Penelope put them on the windowsill. When there were so many letters on the windowsill that they began to fall back onto the floor, she threw most of them away without opening them. The rest of them she took out to the barn. Henry didn't know if she opened them there or not. After that first morning he never went into the barn.

He wasn't completely alone all day. There was a housekeeper, Mrs. Regan, who came every day after breakfast. She came in a taxi driven by a man in a check cap. Mrs. Regan went home in the same taxi after cooking the dinner in the evening.

Henry liked Mrs. Regan. She gave him great thick bacon sandwiches for lunch and talked to him. Henry tried to talk back, but it was difficult. The trouble was he couldn't understand what Mrs. Regan said. He decided after a day or two that she did speak English, but she made such different sounds of the words that he couldn't recognize them.

It was the same in the village. The village was three miles from the house. Henry could ride there on a bicycle Penelope found for him. There were so many hills that three miles was a long way, and there wasn't much to do in the village when he got there. Sometimes he found a few boys kicking a rubber ball up and down the main street. They smiled and let him kick it too. But he could understand very little that they said to him, and nothing that they said to each other. They didn't seem to want to talk about the same things anyway. They had never heard of the Cheyennes or Tom Sawyer. As far as he could make out, they had never been to a movie. If he tried to tell them about America or his home there, they said, "I know."

There was a little cove half a mile from the house where Henry could swim. The water was so cold there was never anyone else there. The weather was difficult to understand too. Sometimes when the sun was shining he would walk down to the beach and by the time he got there it was raining.

After a few days something started to happen to Henry. He felt lazier than he had felt in school. But that was only part of it. He began to feel younger and younger too.

He started to do things he hadn't done for years.

Childish things.

Four

If you go out with Henry,
Go down any street,
Henry never walks with you.
He skips on prancing feet.

He skips three times around each tree,
Draws zeros in the dust.
And if you ask him why, he says,
"It's just because I must."

If you say, "Come on, Henry,
Don't climb on that door."
He says, "I have to. Can't you see,
That's what this door is for."

"I have to touch this wooden fence.
I have to nod my head.
I have to count to twenty-eight,
Before I go to bed."

Henry's father had written that on a birthday
card for him when Henry was six. Henry's father
taught English at a college in the Hudson Valley and
he liked to make up rhymes. Henry had forgotten the
rest of the words on the birthday card. He had forgotten the rest of the things he did when he walked
down a street. He could only remember that there

was a street light outside the house next door and he couldn't pass the house unless he walked around the street light. He didn't know why any more. It was all a long time ago, when he was six, and he had stopped doing it one day just before he was seven.

Now he started doing things like that again. One morning he told himself he couldn't open the gate unless he touched every one of the bars first. The next day on his way down to the beach he had to count how many steps he took to cross the second field from the house. A hundred and eighty-seven steps. He had to say "a hundred and eighty-seven" five times before he went in swimming.

The most important thing he had to do was to look at the great tall mine chimney at the top of the hill the first thing in the morning.

He could see the chimney easily from his bedroom window. But it's difficult not to open your eyes the moment you wake up. If you do, the first thing you see is your pillow or the wallpaper. Henry had to get out of bed, feel his way across the room, and not open his eyes until he had drawn the curtains. It was a couple of days before he managed to do this. The third day he didn't trip over anything. He found the curtain and pulled it aside with his eyes still shut.

He opened them. There was the chimney. As he looked at it a puff of smoke blew out of the top of it. It was like a signal to tell him he had done it right at last.

As soon as Penelope had gone off to her barn Henry touched every bar in the gate. He didn't open the gate. He had to climb over it. He ran up the hill to the chimney.

At first he wasn't sure what he had to do when he

got there. He walked around the bottom of the chimney looking at it. It took twenty-eight steps before he got back to where he had started. There was a large white stone there, as big as a bicycle wheel. It was set among the smaller, rougher stones the chimney was built with.

As he looked at it Henry knew what he had to do. He had to walk around the chimney five times and every time he came back to that stone he had to kick it.

He didn't do it at once. He remembered what Penelope had told him. "The idiots think there are ghosts in the copper mine." Henry had never seen a ghost. A boy at school said *he* had. "It was like a cloud with a face and hands," he told everyone. Henry believed him.

What's so frightening about a cloud with a face and hands? Henry asked himself. What could it do to you? He knew what it could do. It could wrap itself around him.

He began to walk slowly around the bottom of the chimney. After twenty-eight steps he was back at the big white stone. He kicked it. He walked around again. Another kick. He counted each time he came back to the stone.

Three.

Kick.

Four.

Kick.

Five.

Kick.

He could see at once he had done the right thing. The stone swung slowly away from him. It opened like a door. Henry lay down on the ground and looked into the hole where the stone had been. He couldn't see anything. He crawled forward a little. He tried to look up, but he couldn't stretch his neck back far enough to see the light at the top of the chimney unless he crawled forward a little farther.

He was only halfway through the hole when he lost his balance.

It was a horrible feeling.

There was nothing under him. He was falling, turning over and over in space.

He was falling into a long, black nowhere.

Five

HENRY landed on his back.

He had fallen out of a tree at home last summer so he knew what to expect. He could see the same lights rushing at him now. It was like driving along a highway at night when it's snowing. The snowflakes spin out of the darkness at you, bright as flames in the headlights.

The worst part was that all the breath was knocked out of him. He had to struggle to gasp any air back inside his chest.

The grass tickling his face made him feel better. He hadn't landed on hard rock. It wasn't long before he was sure he hadn't broken his back or a leg or anything.

All he could see was a little circle of light a long way up. He guessed it was the top of the chimney.

"Kevin?"

It was a soft voice. It sounded like a girl's. It came from behind him.

"Kevin?" The voice was closer.

Henry sat up.

He could just see her as she knelt in the grass a foot away. She was about the same age as he was, he thought. She had a thin white face with a straight nose. Her black hair was plaited into thick pigtails that hung down to her waist.

She looked like one of the children from the village. Except for her dress. It had a high neck and long sleeves.

Except for her eyes too, Henry noticed. She had the biggest, darkest eyes he had ever seen.

When Henry looked at her, she shook her head. He could tell she was disappointed about something.

"Where's Kevin?"

Henry tried to answer but he still didn't have enough breath to speak.

"How did you know the signal?"

"Wha ignal?" It was all Henry could manage to get out.

"Can you understand me?"

Henry nodded. She didn't talk like Mrs. Regan or the people in the village. She talked like the wives of Henry the Eighth he had seen on television at home.

"You knocked five times. We thought it was Kevin. We've been expecting him back for weeks. That's why we opened the door."

"I didn't know it was a signal." Henry could whisper now.

The girl stood up. Her dress reached down to her ankles. "You'd better come and meet the others. We'll have to decide what to do with you. Can you see the way?"

He could see a small circle of grass in the faint light from the top of the chimney. He could just see the girl standing at the edge of the circle. There was nothing beyond it except darkness.

"No," Henry said.

"Wait here."

He heard her moving away through the grass.

There was a tiny flare in the blackness. He watched the girl coming back toward him. She was carrying a lighted candle.

"Come on."

She walked off. Henry followed her. He did his best to stay close to the candle.

"Look out for the tree here."

"Squeeze your way between these rocks."

"Be careful crossing the bridge."

Henry did everything she told him. It was like looking at pictures one after the other. Sometimes the light of the candle shone for a moment on the bark of a tree. Sometimes on the wet face of a rock. The railing of a foot bridge. Once into the dark opening of a cave.

"Watch out for the Ulalus."

That was when they passed the cave. Henry couldn't see any Ulalus, whatever they were. But he thought he could hear them breathing. It was a deep, unpleasant sound.

"Now mind going down the stairs."

Henry watched his own feet. He counted each time he put one of them below the other. The stairs had been cut out of rock. They went one way for a few yards and then twisted back and went the other way. The steps were smooth and blue green.

A hundred and eighty-five. A hundred and eighty-six.

"It's just across the field now."

A hundred and eighty-seven steps. That was a long way down. The grass was up to his waist as he walked on across level ground. The air felt fresher. There was a slight breeze. It was still as dark as ever except for the flickering candle. But he didn't feel he was inside any longer. It was like walking across any field at night when there is no moon and no stars.

"Wait here."

Henry saw a blue wooden door. She opened it and disappeared. Henry was left alone in the moonless night. He heard soft footsteps. Whispers. A man said something he didn't understand. The next moment everything was lighted up.

He was standing outside a small stone cottage with a straw roof. The light came from two windows, one on each side of the door.

The door opened and the girl told him to come in.

Six

IT was very bright inside the house with that special important light candles make when a lot of them are burning at the same time. Like a birthday cake.

That was all Henry could see at first. Bit by bit he saw other things. A table. Wooden chairs. A bench along the wall. A picture of a young man hanging above it. Logs smouldering in a fireplace.

The girl pushed him forward into the room. He could see everything now. In the corner by the fireplace three people were standing, watching him.

They were less frightening than Henry had expected. They were all smiling. The girl told him who they were.

"Johnchristopher and Hester and Martin."

Martin was about two years younger than Henry. His hair was cut in a straight line above his eyes. He was wearing short trousers and long woolen socks.

Johnchristopher was older than Henry's father. He had on a black suit buttoned up to his shirt collar. When he smiled his teeth stuck out like a small white fan.

Hester wasn't as tall as Penelope but she looked just as strong. Her gray dress covered her all the way down to the floor.

All their clothes looked new. All three of them had the same huge dark eyes as the girl who had led him here.

"I'm Shana O'Neill," the girl said.

"Henry Travers. How do you do?" It was what his father said when he met someone he didn't know. His own name first and then, "How do you do?" Henry had never tried it before.

It was like turning on a radio. Johnchristopher and Hester and Martin all started talking as fast as they could. The sounds they made weren't like the up-and-down words Mrs. Regan used when she spoke English. They were like nothing Henry had ever heard before.

"Can you understand?" Shana asked him.

"No."

Shana made some of the same weird sounds. Johnchristopher and Hester and Martin stopped. The four of them moved closer to Henry, joining hands to make a circle around him.

They all closed their enormous eyes.

"Can you understand now?" Johnchristopher asked. He didn't seem to be able to say anything without smiling.

"Yes."

"We thought you could. We thought anybody could understand us even if we're speaking Irish, and . . ."

"Shut up, Martin," Shana told him. "We don't know anything about him yet."

"He's only a young boy. What harm could he do us? Come and sit at the table." Hester pulled out a chair. "You'll have a piece of cake." She moved away. When she came back she was holding a plate with a piece of cake on it. Henry didn't see where she had got it from.

"He could do us a lot of harm." Shana sat down

facing Henry. He started to eat the cake. It had raisins and cherries in it. "He could tell people outside about us."

"Not if we don't want him to." Martin sat down too.

"We can't stop him saying anything he likes outside."

"Shana's right." Johnchristopher pulled out a bench for himself and Hester. "Kevin told us that. We must never try to change anything outside."

"They already know about you."

Henry wasn't sure why he said it. He didn't like the way they kept talking about "outside." They made it sound so far away. Saying people knew about them seemed to bring everyday things, his room and the gate and the bicycle, closer.

"What do they know?" Shana grabbed his wrist as he was lifting the last bite of cake to his mouth.

"They see smoke coming out the chimney. So they know there's someone down here . . . in here . . . wherever we are." He had come such a long twisting way with Shana, Henry wasn't sure where he was.

"We'll have to think about that smoke." Hester looked at the fireplace.

"We'll think about it later." Shana let go of Henry's wrist. "Do they know who we are?"

"They think you're ghosts."

"We're not ghosts." Henry had never seen anyone get excited as quickly as Martin did. He was jumping up and down, flipping his hands like a seal. "We're not ghosts," he shouted. "We're not."

"Of course we're not." Hester put her arm around him and made him sit down.

"He said people think we are."

"It doesn't matter what other people think. Remember what Kevin told us. It's only what *we* think that counts."

Henry had heard his father say the same thing. He had never believed his father meant it. He believed Hester did, though. He finished his cake.

"All right," Shana said. "Now tell us all about yourself."

"Yes."

"Come on, Henry."

"Please."

They were all leaning toward him, watching him with their great dark eyes.

They waited for him to begin.

Seven

IT was what Henry had wanted for a long time. All last winter at home and ever since the air hostess had left him with Penelope. One person who didn't look puzzled or bored when he said anything. One person who wanted to know about him.

Now he had four of them at once. Four people waiting to listen to every word.

He couldn't think of anything to say.

They already knew his name. He could tell them where he had been born. South Dakota. When he was four his parents moved to the Hudson Valley. His father taught in a college. His mother went to meetings in New York. Henry went to school.

It was all so dull. He had never done anything in his life. He had just been moved from one place to another. He was only in Ireland because his parents had sent him here.

"I come from a town on the banks of the Mississippi River," Henry began. "It's a one-horse town. I live with my Aunt Polly. She's awfully strict. She won't let me go swimming. She sews up my shirts. But I can fool her. I just play hooky and do what I like. . . ."

He told them about walking barefoot along the dusty little streets where it was always summer. About the rafts and the great paddle steamers sweeping down the river to New Orleans. He told them about his adventures with his friend, Huck Finn. About Injun Joe digging up the body in the graveyard and murdering the young doctor.

He told them the whole story of Tom Sawyer. He didn't tell it as well as the book did. He forgot bits and made up others. But he managed to give them a fine, lively picture of what it was like in Hannibal, Missouri.

The one thing he didn't say was that the picture he gave them was what it was like over a hundred years ago. He told them about things there as though they had happened last week and nothing had changed since then.

"After Huck and I found the buried treasure in the cave," Henry finished, "I decided to go off and see the world. So I came to Ireland. And here I am."

There was a long silence.

Henry wished he could take it all back. He didn't think they had read the book. They would have stopped him if they had. But they must know he was a liar anyway. He had left out so many everyday things. Things that made the adventures of Tom Sawyer impossible these days. Cars and telephones and electricity.

Henry sat there waiting for Johnchristopher and Hester and Shana and Martin to ask him why there weren't any of those things where he came from.

Eight

"IT sounds like a grand place." Hester said at last.

"We almost went to America once," Johnchristopher told Henry.

"Kevin wanted to go," Shana explained. "He was going to take us all with him."

"But then after Kevin stole the sheep . . ." Hester's voice trailed off.

"We had to come down here," Shana finished for her.

"Stole the sheep?" Henry wanted them to go on talking about themselves so that they wouldn't ask him why there were no cars in Missouri. It wasn't only that, though. He was interested.

"Why did Kevin steal a sheep?" he asked.

"To keep us alive."

"Keep you alive?"

Shana nodded. "There was nothing else to eat."

"The potatoes went bad."

"The plants turned black in the fields."

"You could smell them rotting all across the land."

"Everyone was starving."

Henry could see they didn't like to remember it. None of them could say more than a few words at a time. They had to keep helping each other along.

"We found John Brien dead in his own field."

"His tongue was all green."

"From eating grass."

"Kevin gave us everything he had."

"He sold his house to help feed the rest of us."

"When there was nothing left he stole the sheep."

"We stewed it." It was the first time Johnchristopher had smiled since they started telling Henry their story.

"We couldn't eat all the bones so we buried them under the fireplace."

"The soldiers found them when they pulled the house down."

"Martin managed to run away."

"That's how I knew," Shana explained. "Then I told Kevin."

"He came and rescued Hester and me from the soldiers."

"They were taking us into town to lock us up."

"Then we all ran away." Martin smiled too, remembering that part.

"Kevin knew a way into the old copper mine. He brought us down here."

"To hide from the soldiers until it's safe to go back outside."

That seemed to be the end of their story. No one said anything else. Henry was even more interested now.

"How do you get things to eat down here?" he asked.

"We ate mushrooms at first."

"There was enough to last us for weeks."

"Thousands and thousands of mushrooms in this mine," Johnchristopher agreed.

Henry remembered the piece of cake Hester had given him.

"Is that all?" he asked. "Did you make that cake out of mushrooms?"

"I did not." Hester looked shocked. "I made it out of flour and butter and eggs and raisins and cherries."

"We began to feel funny after a while," Shana explained. "Eating nothing but mushrooms. Then Kevin had an idea, and he taught us how to think up other things to eat."

"Anything we want," Martin said. Shana glanced at him quickly. "Well, a lot of things, anyway . . ."

Martin's voice ended in a long silence. Henry didn't want to question them about anything they didn't like to remember. But there was one thing he was longing to know.

"What happened to Kevin?"

"I wish we knew that," Hester said sadly.

"He's only been gone a few weeks." Johnchristopher smiled as though telling her not to worry.

"He went outside to see if it's safe for us to leave yet," Shana explained.

"To find out if the soldiers are still looking for us."

Henry hadn't seen any soldiers in this part of Ireland, but there was a policeman in the village. Henry had seen him digging in his garden.

"The potatoes are all right now," he said cheerfully. "We have them for dinner every night. Usually boiled."

"That's the best way," Hester agreed. "Boiled in their skins."

Henry liked them better French fried. He didn't say so. He had a sudden idea.

"Shall I try to find Kevin for you?" he suggested. "I could ask if anyone's seen him in the village."

"No." Shana could get excited almost as quickly as Martin. "You'll give him away. Once they know he's out there, they'll hunt him down. If they can't capture him, they'll shoot him."

"I expect he's staying safely hidden in the daytime all right." Hester got Shana to sit down again.

"Traveling by night," Martin said.

"He'll be back any day now," Johnchristopher added.

"Of course he will." Shana was still excited. "Next week at the latest."

"This is Kevin." Hester showed Henry the picture of a young man that was hanging on the wall. "Kevin O'Neill. We thought we'd like to have a picture of him."

Henry walked over and looked at it. Kevin O'Neill had a thin face and a straight nose like Shana's. His eyes weren't like Shana's though. They were the ordinary size. He was smiling with one side of his mouth. There was something about him that made Henry sure that wherever he was Kevin was all right. He looked as if he had never been frightened of anything in his life.

"You'll stay and have dinner with us." Hester unhooked an iron pot that was hanging over the fire.

"What is it?" Martin asked.

"What would you like, Martin?"

"I think I'd like lamb stew."

"That's what you'll get then." Hester smiled at Henry. "Would you like lamb stew too?"

Henry was going to say, "Yes, please. Lamb stew would be fine." Then he remembered that Penelope was taking him out somewhere tonight. He had no idea what the time was. But if Hester was getting dinner it must be after six.

"I'm afraid I'd better go now." He turned to Shana. "Will you show me the way back to the chimney?" He was sure he could never find it alone.

Shana didn't move.

"Go on, Shana," Hester told her.

Shana still didn't move.

"I don't think we ought to let him go," she said at last.

Nine

"WHY ever not, Shana?" Hester asked.

"He'll tell people about us."

"I won't."

"If they find out we're hiding here, they'll come down and arrest us."

"I won't. I won't tell anyone about you."

"I still think he'd better stay." Shana looked at the others to see what they thought. "At least until Kevin gets back."

"That won't be long."

"He'll probably come tonight."

"We'll think up a nice place for you to sleep," Hester promised.

There were several reasons why Henry wanted to leave. He wanted to get "outside" again. Out in the daylight. Back to things he was used to. He wanted to sit down and think about everything that had happened. There was another reason that had nothing to do with him. Even Penelope would notice he wasn't there sooner or later. Mrs. Regan would anyway. And he was worried about *them*, about Shana and the others. About Kevin on the run out there.

"If I don't go home they'll come looking for me," he explained. "I walked around the mine chimney five times this morning. They might find my footsteps. They might come down here after me."

They all nodded except Shana. They obviously thought Henry was right. At last Shana nodded too. She stood up.

"Come on."

Henry said good-bye to each of the others in turn.

He said he'd like to come back if they'd let him. They said they'd be pleased to see him any time.

It was still moonless night outside the cottage. Shana led him a little way off through the long grass. She stopped. Henry stopped too. He could just see her face in the light from the candles shining out through the cottage windows.

There was something about her he had only half noticed before.

"You look like Kevin," he said.

"Why shouldn't I? He's my brother."

"Johnchristopher and Hester. Are they your parents?"

"I haven't any parents." Her face was very serious. "But Johnchristopher and the others are Kevin's best friends. If anything happens to them, or to me, Kevin'll hear about it."

Shana didn't say what Kevin would do then. She didn't have to. Henry remembered the thin face in the picture.

"I won't tell anyone about you."

Shana still looked serious.

"I promise." There was no one in the world Henry wanted to tell.

"All right." Shana made up her mind to believe him. "You can go now if you like."

"Aren't you going to show me the way . . . ?"
Henry looked into the blackness around him.

"Hold out your hands."

Henry did.

"Close your eyes."

Henry closed his eyes. He felt her thin dry hands clasp his. She had a very strong grip. His fingers were all bunched up. He tried to straighten them.

The next moment something so extraordinary happened that he could never tell anyone about it as long as he lived.

Suddenly—

He—

Himself—

Henry—

Just wasn't there.

Ten

THERE was the beach. And the cove. And above it the hill. And the chimney against the evening sky.

The tide was out. It was raining gently.

Then bit by bit Henry was there too. There were his hands and his feet. There was all the rest of his body that he could usually see. He could feel the rain on his face so his head was there too.

Henry sat down for a minute to think about it. He picked out a flat pebble and skipped it over the sea. It bounced five times before it sank.

He was not only there. He was as good as new.

He started to walk back to the house.

There were three fresh looping tracks in the mud outside the gate. The taxi had come and turned around and taken Mrs. Regan home.

Penelope was sitting in her usual chair in the living room listening to the clinking in her head.

"We'd better go," she said when she noticed Henry. "The Lieutenant's expecting us at seven."

It was about four miles along a winding road by the sea to The Lieutenant's house. Henry kept looking out of the car window for soldiers. He didn't see any. He did see pieces of stone wall in some of the fields that looked like houses that had been pulled down. The few people they passed looked cheerful enough, though. None of them was eating grass.

They went between two old stone gate posts.

Past a dock with a sailboat tied up to it. Under some trees with branches like feathers.

"Cypresses," Penelope said.

She stopped the car in front of an old house that seemed to wander off in every direction. Parts of it looked as if they might fall down without any soldiers having to pull them.

A very old man opened the door. He had white hair growing out of his ears. It was almost the only hair he had. Henry followed Penelope into a big hall with a staircase curving up from it. He looked around for The Lieutenant. He had seen lieutenants in the movies. Sometimes they were young and yelled "Come on" and captured a lot of Germans or Japanese. Sometimes they were even younger and just said "Yes, sir" when someone told them what to do. Then they went off to do it and you never saw them again.

"This is The Lieutenant, Lieutenant Claire," Penelope said.

The old man shook Henry's hand.

"This is my nephew, Henry . . . Henry . . ."

"Henry Travers. How do you do?"

"Travers, of course," Penelope remembered.

"How do you do, Henry?" The Lieutenant led the way into another room. It had a lot of tall windows looking out over a lawn and the sea.

"Where's Jane?" Penelope asked.

"She'll be arriving in Skibbereen . . ." The Lieutenant took a round watch out of his pocket. "In about twelve minutes. Unless the bus is late."

"Aren't you going to meet her?"

"My car broke down the day after Christmas. I haven't been able to get it started since then."

"You old fox. So that's why you invited me to dinner."

The Lieutenant did look a little like an old fox, Henry decided. A very old fox. He had the same pointed face and bright eyes.

"If you'd had the decency to call me," Penelope was saying, "I could have picked Jane up on the way here."

"If I'd called you, you wouldn't have answered the phone. The only way I could get you here was to send a message with Murphy's taxi."

"Oh, all right. But give me a drink first."

Henry stopped listening again. He had thought of something. If this old man was a lieutenant he must have been in the army. He might still have friends who were soldiers. He might have heard if they were hunting for Kevin. Henry wondered how he could find out if The Lieutenant knew anything without giving Kevin away.

There was the sound of Penelope's car outside as she drive off to meet Jane at the bus station. Henry was alone with the old man.

"How do you like Ireland?" The Lieutenant was sitting in a big chair with sides to it. Henry could hardly see his face. He was going to say he thought Ireland was great, but he had an idea the old man would know he wasn't telling the truth. Then they'd both start lying to each other. Or they'd talk the way people often did, thinking about something else all the time. Then Henry could never find out anything.

"I guess it's all right. But I get confused here," he admitted. "I can't understand what the people are saying most of the time, and if I try to tell them anything they say they know."

42

The Lieutenant laughed. "When the Irish say they know," he explained, "they don't mean they *know*. They mean they understand."

Henry was glad to hear that. At least the boys in the village could understand him even if he couldn't understand them. He wondered why he had found it so easy to understand Shana and the others.

He decided to try to get the talk as close to his friends in the copper mine as he could without saying anything about them.

"The Irish have to eat grass sometimes, don't they?" he asked.

"Eat grass?"

"When the potatoes go rotten and you can smell them all across the land and . . . people . . . steal sheep."

"Who told you about that?" Henry still couldn't see The Lieutenant's face. His voice sounded angry and sad.

"Friends." It was as much as Henry could say without lying.

"The Irish have never forgotten that. They never will." Henry could tell The Lieutenant meant he would never forget it either.

"Why did the soldiers pull their houses down?"

"Because the people couldn't pay their rents." The Lieutenant's voice seemed to come out of the darkness. "It was a terrible time. A terrible, cruel time."

"Did you eat grass?"

"Me?"

"When the potatoes went bad."

"My dear boy." The Lieutenant laughed. He got up and poured some more whiskey into his glass.

"I'm not *that* old. All that was during the great famine. I wasn't even born then."

"You weren't born?" Henry leaned forward staring into the old man's face.

"It was over a hundred years ago."

Eleven

A FEW words at a time, while they waited for Penelope to come back with Jane, The Lieutenant told Henry more about it.

The barefooted crowds waiting all day for a handful of Indian corn. The families living in the ditches after their houses had been pulled down. Even when they managed to earn a few pennies working on the roads, there was no food in the shops. The women carrying their dead children in their arms. So many people falling and dying in the streets there was no one to bury them. The way their eyes looked, huge and dark with hunger.

Henry wanted to hear about it. But he was so puzzled and shocked his attention kept wandering. He kept thinking about Shana.

He could see one possible reason she had never asked him why there were no cars in Missouri.

He could see why she might have believed everything he told her about the town Tom Sawyer lived in, when he described it as though it was still like that today, with no electricity or telephones.

If she and the others had hidden in the copper mine during the great famine, and they had been hiding down there ever since, she wouldn't know that anything had changed outside. She didn't know about electricity or any of those things.

But that meant Shana—

It had to mean Shana—

Was over a hundred years old.

What was even more puzzling and extraordinary was that Henry didn't think she knew it.

She talked about hiding in the mine as though it had all happened last month. She thought the soldiers were still looking for them.

He remembered what Shana had said about the mushrooms.

"We began to feel funny after a while, eating nothing but mushrooms."

Henry had read about Indians doing that. The Cheyennes had eaten mushrooms sometimes and they had done weird things afterwards. They had believed all kinds of impossible things. They thought they could walk into the enemy's camp without being seen. They thought no bullet could kill them.

He had never read that any of them had lived to be over a hundred without growing any older. Without *looking* any older. But maybe they had.

"We were lucky. My family managed to get away to America," The Lieutenant was saying. "My grandfather did well there. In the West. He came back to Ireland and bought this house and the land. My mother was his only child. She married here and our family's lived here ever since. I was born here. So was my son. So was Jane."

Henry heard Penelope's car outside. The Lieutenant stood up. Penelope came into the room with a young girl.

The Lieutenant kissed her. "This is my granddaughter, Jane. Jane Claire," he told Henry.

Henry wanted to say, "Henry Travers. How do you do?"

He couldn't. He couldn't say anything. He could only stare at the girl.

Jane Claire was about the same age as he was. She had a thin face with a small straight nose. Her black hair was plaited into two thick pigtails that hung down to her waist.

She looked exactly like Shana.

Twelve

THEY had lamb stew for dinner. Penelope drank several glasses of wine. It made her different. It seemed to stop the clinking in her head. She talked to people instead of past them. She asked Jane about her mother, Henrietta, in London. She asked who Henrietta was married to now. She listened to the answers. She didn't interrupt when Jane told Henry about the islands in Roaring Water Bay.

Henry was interested in the islands. Ever since he had first seen them from the top of the hill by the chimney he had wanted to explore them. The far islands were the best, Jane said.

Henry kept watching her. She didn't look *exactly* like Shana. Her eyes weren't as big or as dark. She didn't talk like Shana either. Her mother had been born in America and Jane said "okay" and "lousy." Shana never used those words.

After dinner Jane wanted to go and look at her sailboat.

Henry went with her. They sat on the dock, their legs dangling over the still water.

"You can sail all the way to Cape Clear with a southwest wind."

"Which one is Cape Clear?"

Jane pointed to the farthest of the islands.

"How long does it take to sail there?" Henry

wanted to keep her talking. It gave him a chance to look for other ways in which she was different from Shana. He wanted her to be different. He didn't know why.

"It's great being back here," Jane said after a while. "With the whole summer ahead. My mother keeps getting married so I spend most of the time in lousy boarding schools in England. Holidays here with The Lieutenant are the only things I look forward to."

"Why do they call him The Lieutenant?" Henry asked. "Was he in the army?"

"No." Jane shook her head. "Not the ordinary army, anyway. The whole family's always been very . . . Irish," she explained. "My great-great-grandfather was the commanding general of all the rebel forces around here. When he died Grandfather took over from him. He was so young at the time they used to call him The Lieutenant. And people have been calling him that ever since. He's told me wonderful stories about fighting the British. Setting ambushes for them and smuggling in guns." She was silent for a minute looking at the water. It was beginning to get dark. "I wish he wasn't quite so old. It'd be awful if he died. He's the only family I've got."

Henry asked her what had happened to her father.

"He had an accident with a shotgun."

That started Henry talking about his parents. He told Jane he had to write separate letters to them every week. One to his father in Black Mountain and one to his mother in New York.

"I just write one letter and copy it out again," he

said. "Then I can be sure I'm telling them both the same things."

"I know," Jane agreed. "You have to be awfully careful with parents about things like that. Mother's always saying she hopes I like her new husbands. But she gets mad if I tell them anything I haven't told her."

"Mine used to be all right," Henry remembered. "I think the trouble started when they stopped listening to each other."

It was only when he was in bed that night, waiting to go to sleep, that Henry happened to remember that he had never for a moment thought of telling Jane lies about himself. He hadn't made up a lot of stories about his life back home the way he had with Shana.

He had wanted to tell Jane the truth.

Thirteen

HENRY didn't bother to walk around and around the chimney the next morning. He kicked the big white stone, counted up to twenty-eight, and then kicked it again. When he had kicked it five times it swung away from him. He crawled into the hole where it had been.

He was careful not to crawl too far and lose his balance. But there was no danger of that this time. As soon as he got his head through the hole, he saw it was light inside the chimney. There was a ring of candles at the bottom of the cave. Shana was standing in the center of the ring. She pointed to an old iron ladder hanging down into the mine. Henry managed to swing himself onto it.

Shana was wearing a new dress. It had the same long sleeves and a skirt down to her ankles, but it was white instead of blue.

"I think I'd better close the door," she said as Henry stepped off the last rung of the ladder. He looked up. The white stone swung back into place.

"Did any of the soldiers see you come down here?"

"No."

"You're sure?"

"Yes."

Henry had thought a lot about Shana while he

was having breakfast. He had decided for certain that neither she nor the others had any idea how much time had passed since they had hidden in the mine. Everything they had said to him proved that.

Walking up the hill to the chimney he had tried to put himself in their place. How would he like to be told all of a sudden that he was over a hundred years old?

He had made up his mind not to say anything about it to Shana or Johnchristopher or any of them.

"Watch out for the Ulalus." They were passing the opening to the cave near the top of the steps.

"What are Ulalus?" Henry stopped, listening to the deep unpleasant breathing from the darkness inside.

"They're like wolves. Enormous black wolves. They're bigger than horses." Shana was listening too. "They eat people," she added.

"Aren't you afraid of them?" Henry walked on. He walked as fast as he could without running.

"Of course." Shana caught up with him.

"Aren't you afraid they'll come out and eat you?"

"We don't think the Ulalus can get out of the cave."

"Why not?"

"We don't think they know how to."

They reached the top of the steps. It all looked different from last time. For one thing it was daylight. It looked like daylight, anyway, although there wasn't any sun. Henry could see he was standing near the top of a huge cave. It was bigger than the inside of any building he had ever seen. Bigger than Radio City Music Hall. Far below was the great field and the stone cottage. Johnchristopher was plowing the field with a hand plow. Hester was leading the horse and Martin was walking behind it. They all looked very small from where he was standing.

He glanced up at the roof of the cave. It looked almost like the sky. It was a great dome, the same blue green color as the steps he had walked down yesterday.

Was it yesterday? Henry wondered. It didn't seem as long ago as that. If he hadn't known that he had gone to The Lieutenant's house and met Jane and gone home and slept and had breakfast, he would have thought it was only a few minutes, no time at all, since he had stood outside the cottage with Shana. Since he had suddenly found he wasn't there.

He looked back down at the field where the others were plowing. The long grass he had walked through yesterday had all been cut short. It hadn't been left lying on the ground. It had been gathered and built into a neat haystack beside the cottage. He wondered how they had found time to do that. Unless they had worked all night.

"When did you cut the grass?" he asked Shana.

"Johnchristopher wanted to plow the field, so we thought it had better be scythed and stacked."

"Didn't it take a long time?"

Shana didn't answer at once. She was looking straight at Henry. She seemed to be searching him with her eyes before she made up her mind about something.

"We didn't have to do it ourselves," she said at last. "Johnchristopher doesn't like cutting grass. Neither does Hester. So we just decided to think we'd done it."

Whenever Henry had a lot of questions darting about inside his mind, he had to sit down. He couldn't sort them out standing up. He sat down on the top step looking out over the field and the cottage below.

He remembered that when he had first met Johnchristopher and Hester and Martin he couldn't understand a word they said. Then they all joined hands and made a ring around him. The next moment they were all talking English as clearly as people back home.

"We thought you could understand us," Martin said.

They all used that word "think" a lot.

"We'll have to think about that," Hester said when Henry told her about the smoke coming out of the chimney.

"We began to feel funny after a while eating nothing but mushrooms," Shana said later. "Then Kevin had an idea and taught us how to think up other things to eat."

They used it whenever they wanted anything.

"I think I'd like lamb stew."

"We thought we'd like to have a picture of Kevin."

"We'll think up a nice place for you to sleep."

"I think I'd better close the door."

"We don't think the Ulalus can get out of the cave."

For the first time Henry noticed a small clear stream running beside the house and away across the field. Johnchristopher had stopped plowing. He was kneeling by the stream cupping water into his mouth with his hands.

"Did Johnchristopher just think he'd like a drink of water?" Henry asked Shana.

"I expect so."

"Can you . . . ?" It seemed too wonderful to be possible. "Can you think up anything you want?"

Shana nodded. "Almost anything."

"You just think it's there? Or it's done? Or you've got it?"

"Yes."

"Can you stop things if you want to, too?"

"Yes."

Then why didn't they stop the Ulalus? he wondered. They didn't think they could get out of their cave. But they were still there. They still made that unpleasant, threatening sound every time anyone passed by.

"Why don't you just think there *aren't* any Ulalus?" Henry asked.

Fourteen

"YOU can't have hot unless you have cold," Johnchristopher explained.

"Or good without bad," Hester said.

"Or play without work," Martin put in.

"Or rest without being tired," Hester went on.

"Or kindness without cruelty," Shana added.

They were all sitting around the table in the cottage eating cake and drinking milk. The moment they saw Henry they thought the horse could finish the job alone. Henry could see it through the window pulling the plow in long straight furrows across the field.

"So you can't have safety unless there's danger, can you?" Shana asked him. "That's why we think the Ulalus are there. So there's something we can feel safe from."

"It was Kevin's idea," Hester remembered. "He thought the Ulalus were there before he left."

Henry could see it made sense. He finished his milk. It was cool and fresh. But he wouldn't have enjoyed it if he hadn't been thirsty.

Hester filled his cup again from a stone jug. Henry thanked her. There was one more question darting about in his mind. There was one thing they all wanted and didn't have. It was there like a sigh behind everything they said.

"Why don't you *think* Kevin here?" he asked. "Why don't you just *think* he's come back?"

There was a silence. They all glanced at each other, waiting to see who wanted to tell him.

"Because Kevin's outside," Shana answered at last.

"And that's one thing Kevin always told us," Johnchristopher said quietly. "We must never change anything outside."

Henry didn't understand.

"Why not?" he asked.

"Because it could change everything."

"Other people's lives."

"And we wouldn't know we were doing it."

"Or how we were doing it."

"Until it was too late."

"So it's wrong to interfere." They were all helping each other along again.

"Do you see?" Hester asked.

"Suppose you only changed things for the better," Henry suggested. "Suppose . . ." He tried to find an idea that would make sense to them. "Suppose you decided to think people outside were growing wonderful potatoes. The best potato crop they've ever had. And they did. What harm could that do?"

None of them answered. They were all looking at Shana, waiting for her to tell him.

"Fifty years from now," Shana said slowly, "it might change the whole world."

"How?"

"There might be a young man on a farm somewhere who was planning to go to America." Shana was talking faster now. "In America he might meet a girl and get married. They might have a son, and fifty years from now their son might be . . . Well, he could be . . ."

"President of the United States," Martin said.

"Yes," Shana agreed. "And if there was a wonderful potato crop this year . . ."

"The Irish never leave Ireland," Johnchristopher started to point out.

"When there's a good crop," Hester finished for him.

"You see now?" Shana asked Henry. "If that young man doesn't go to America. You see how it could change *everything?*"

Henry did. Once you started to change something, you could never be sure where it was going to end.

He still couldn't quite see what that had to do with Kevin, though.

"But if you just thought Kevin was back," he said.

"We don't know what Kevin's doing now." Shana was speaking for all of them again. "He might be helping someone to escape from the English soldiers. This very moment. Or up in the hills with the men on the run."

"Perhaps one of them's wounded." The hair over Martin's eyes was waving up and down like a plume as he nodded with excitement. "And Kevin's binding up his leg, trying to stop the blood."

"Or he might be arranging for us all to go to America." Hester looked excited too.

"Talking to the captain of the ship about smuggling us on board," Johnchristopher agreed.

Henry didn't think any of these things were very likely. He didn't believe there were any English soldiers to escape from any more. At least not in this part of Ireland. He didn't believe there were any desperate wounded men up in the hills around here either. He had climbed Mount Gabriel, the biggest hill for miles, one day when he had nothing else to do. The only things he had seen on the run up there were sheep. And if Kevin was arranging for them all to go to America he was more likely to be in the travel office in Skibbereen than talking to the captain of a ship.

Henry nodded. He couldn't say any of this. He had decided not to tell them how much things had changed outside since they had been in the mine. He could see what they meant about Kevin, anyway.

If Kevin was driving along a road, and they suddenly thought him back here, the car could roll on without him until it hit something—or somebody.

Something dangerous could happen if you stopped anyone doing anything, all at once, without warning.

Henry started to swallow his last bite of cake. When it was halfway down he pretended that Shana suddenly thought he had stopped swallowing. Hester had to thump him on the back to keep him from choking.

"If we only knew where Kevin was," he said. "You could send him a message and just ask him to come back."

"Yes." Shana was looking at him in that searching way that made him feel she was trying to see inside him.

The trouble was they didn't know where to start looking. Henry didn't think they even knew how long Kevin had been gone.

Johnchristopher had said Kevin had left the mine a few weeks ago. Henry didn't believe that meant much. He knew how slippery time could be. The only way you could keep any grip on it was by doing the same things every day.

When he was home Henry took the school bus every morning. He climbed the steps of the bus. The door squeaked open. He stepped into the smell of peanut butter and gasoline. When he had done that five times, the next day was Saturday. It might seem years since Monday. But it wasn't. Because that was how you were sure five days had passed. You counted the number of times you stepped into the same smell and had the same sick feeling. If you stayed home from school with a cold you forgot at once whether it was Tuesday or Wednesday or even what month it was.

Shana and Johnchristopher and Hester and Martin never seemed to do any of the same things at the same time every day.

They didn't even bother to *have* every day.

Walking across the field to the cottage Henry had asked Shana how long the daylight would last.

"As long as we think it will."

"What'll happen then?"

"We'll think it's dark."

If you went on like that, having days and nights just when you happened to think of it, time could stop meaning anything at all. Years could pass without your knowing it. They had passed without Shana or the others growing any older.

As far as Henry could see Kevin might have left the mine any time during the last hundred years.

60

"Yes," Shana said again. She was still looking at Henry in that searching way.

"What?" Henry had forgotten why she had said "yes" the first time.

"We had a talk about you before you came back. We decided we can trust you."

"We know we can." Johnchristopher showed his small white fan of teeth in a smile.

"You'll have to be careful, of course."

"For your own sake too," Hester put in.

"Traveling by night," Martin suggested.

"Henry doesn't have to go on the run, Martin." Shana turned back to Henry. "You'll just have to ask a lot of questions without anyone guessing why you're asking them."

"Questions?" Henry had a slight anxious feeling. It was like the way he felt when he was stepping up to bat.

"We want you to find Kevin for us."

Fifteen

WHEN Henry got back to the gate that evening Mrs. Regan was just leaving. Mr. Murphy, the taxi driver, had a message for him.

"Only it's raining will you cycle over to The Lieutenant's tomorrow and you and Jane will go to the islands."

Henry was beginning to understand more and more of what the Irish said to him. He thanked Mr. Murphy and walked on to the house. Penelope hadn't come in from her barn yet. There were several letters which the postman had pushed under the door that morning. Henry looked to see if there was one from his mother in New York or his father in Black Mountain. There was only one letter with an American stamp on it. The printing on the envelope said it was from the Bonoco Co., Inc., in Montana. It was addressed to Miss Penelope Fallon. Urgent.

Henry put the letters back on the floor. He sat down. He had a lot to think about.

He and Shana had explored miles and miles of the copper mine that day. It was impossible to explore it all because any of the tunnels they wandered into would go on as long as Shana thought it did. It would twist and turn and go up and down as she liked. When Shana thought they had come to the end of it they would find themselves anywhere she thought they were. In a small cave with a rug on the floor, rocking chairs to sit in, pictures on the wall, books on the shelves. Or in a huge cavern with a clump of trees and a warm stream to swim in. She thought it was daylight in some of the tunnels. In some of them she thought it was dark.

She was always careful not to change anything outside. If she thought there was a stream, she had to think where it went to. Around and around inside the mine, or back into the ground. She had to be sure it didn't break out and flood someone's field on its way to the sea. It was the same with fire. If she thought she'd like a fire in any of the caves, she had to think about the smoke. If she didn't, it might find its own way back through all those miles of tunnels into the big chimney on the hill and puff out of the top where people could see it.

Henry thought it would be great to find a movie house at the end of some tunnel. He was careful not to say so. Shana could only think of things she knew about. She didn't know about films, and Henry wasn't going to tell her. If he did, he would have to tell her about too many other things, about all that had happened, all the years that had passed since she had been in the mine. If Shana ever found out she was over a hundred years old, it wasn't going to be his fault. Henry had decided that once and for all.

They got back to the field and the cottage at last and Henry thought it was time to go home. Shana held his hands and made him close his eyes and little by little he found himself on the beach again.

The moment he did he remembered the last thing she had said to him.

"We're all counting on you to find Kevin for us."

That was what Henry was sitting thinking about now.

Penelope came in from her barn and picked up the mail. Other letters had started falling off the windowsill again. Penelope looked at them. Henry saw there were three other envelopes from the Bonoco Co., Inc., Urgent, amongst them.

Penelope threw them all into the wastepaper basket without opening them.

The phone was ringing. Penelope didn't notice it. She didn't notice Henry either. She sat down and listened to the clinking in her head.

After a moment Henry forgot she was there. There was something clinking in his head too.

Shana's voice.

"Find Kevin."

"Find Kevin."

"Find Kevin."

Sixteen

HENRY had never been in a sailboat before. Jane asked him to handle the jib. The jib was the sail in front. When Jane steered the boat one way the jib had to blow out on the left side of the mast. When she changed direction it had to blow out on the right. Henry had to loosen one rope and tighten another each time. He had to do it quickly, then both he and Jane had to move from one side of the boat to the other. Jane called it "tacking."

After a while Henry got quite good at it and began to enjoy sailing. He could take it easy between tacks and look at the bay and the islands. The sun was shining.

He saw a black leather ball bobbing about on top of the water a long way away. It disappeared. A minute later he saw it in a different place. Jane said it was a seal. They never got close enough to see its face. It never looked like anything but a black leather ball.

They got close to some dolphins. Once Henry counted fourteen dolphins around the boat. They dipped in and out of the sea like roller coasters.

After a lot of tacking they reached the nearest island. Jane steered the boat into shallow water. Henry loosened both ropes at once. They waded ashore onto a sandy beach carrying the anchor and the picnic basket between them. Henry helped Jane force a prong of the anchor into the sand. The boat flapped off away from the shore as far as the anchor rope would let it.

Except for a few sleepy cows Henry and Jane were alone on the island. Jane didn't look so much like Shana today. She was wearing jeans and a blue shirt. Her hair was loose down her back. It smelt fresh and salty. Henry kept wanting to touch it.

It was one of those summer days when everything hums and a leaf or a shell suddenly turns out to be a butterfly. They sat on the beach leaning against a warm rock and ate chicken and sausages and bread and cheese and raw onions. Jane said you had to eat onions at sea or on an island. It stopped you being scurvy. The onions tasted sweet and juicy when you first bit them, then they burnt your tongue like mustard.

"What's the name of the island?" Henry asked.

"Niuatobutabu."

"How do you spell it?"

"It's only called Horse Island on the maps. Grandfather and I named it Niuatobutabu."

"Why?" Henry took a drink of lemonade from the bottle to cool his mouth.

"Mother took me around the world once on one of her honeymoons. When you go from San Francisco to Hong Kong you have to cross something called the International Date Line. It's weird. One day it's Tuesday. And then you cross the line and the next day's Thursday."

"What happens to Wednesday?"

"I don't know. It's just gone. Nobody knows where."

"I know." Henry meant he understood.

"When I asked Grandfather about it he said there was an island in the Pacific called Niuatobutabu where they lose days like that all the time. Because the Date Line goes right through the middle of the island. He made up a rhyme about it."

Jane finished eating a sausage and told Henry the rhyme.

"It's easy to remember,
If Alaska is your home,
When it's Sunday in Amchitka,
It's Saturday in Nome.

But in Niuatobutabu,
If you walk down any street,
They're eating Friday's fish on one side,
And on the other, Thursday's meat.

Every time you cross the fields
You gain or lose a day.
You're older in the cabbages,
And younger in the hay.

Here in lower longitudes,
It's only once a year
We have New Year's Eve and whiskey
Or St. Patrick's Day and beer.

But in Niuatobutabu
All the best days come in pairs,
Because no one knows what day it is,
And no one really cares."

Henry listened to the rhyme without saying anything. He had one of those feelings he got sometimes that everything that was happening to him had happened before.

"The next time Grandfather and I came to Horse Island we decided to rename it Niuatobutabu. Now we can spend a whole weekend here, even if we only stay an hour. And we come over every year on my birthday so I can have two of them."

Part of the feeling was that Henry knew what he wanted to happen next. He wanted to tell Jane he knew someone who wasn't just living in last Tuesday when it was Wednesday here. He knew four people who were living over a hundred years ago. They thought they were anyway, and when they thought something—it was true. Henry had decided there was no one in the world he would ever want to tell about his friends in the copper mine. He wanted to tell Jane about them now. But he had promised Shana . . .

Jane started to collect the scraps of the picnic and put them in the basket. They set out to explore the island.

It was over a mile long. There were clusters of houses at both ends of it. People had lived in them until about twenty years ago, Jane said. They had grown old and moved to the mainland. The houses still had roofs and windows. They explored one of them. The cows had made a smelly mess downstairs, but upstairs the floor was clean and bare. Henry guessed the people must have swept and scrubbed it just before they moved out and left the island. There was a calendar on a wall and a picture of a young woman with a ring around her head over the fireplace. Jane said the young woman was named Mary.

It was so warm and dry in the house Henry and

Jane could have lived in it. He thought about living on the island with Jane. It would be cold in the winter and they could sit by the fire and cook things over it.

Jane was looking out of the window. "The tide's going out," she said. "I'd better go and move the anchor or the boat'll get stuck on the beach."

Henry offered to help her. She said she'd be right back. He sat down on the floor. It was easier to think about living in the house with Jane now that she wasn't there. He decided they would have to bring over a whole lot of food, canned things, and cake, and matches, and blankets, if they were going to stay there all winter. There was a closet in the corner beside the fireplace. He opened it to see if it was big enough to hold all the supplies they would need. There was a basket on the floor under the bottom shelf. Henry pulled it out. It was full of small, light things wrapped in newspaper. He unwrapped one of them. Inside was a seashell, one of those long pointed ones like an Indian tepee. There were different shells in the other pieces of newspaper. Clam shells and oyster and scallop shells and other kinds Henry had never seen before. Someone must have collected them once and put them away and forgotten them.

The next moment Henry forgot the shells too. He caught sight of a name on one of the pieces of newspaper. It was printed in big letters.

"SHANA O'NEILL."

There were other names below it. "JOHNCHRISTOPHER SULLIVAN. HESTER SULLIVAN. MARTIN SULLIVAN."

It said "ANNOUNCEMENT" above the names.

And below them in the same letters, "WILL ANYONE KNOWING THE PRESENT WHEREABOUTS OF THE ABOVE NAMED PERSONS PLEASE GET IN TOUCH WITH MR. KEVIN O'NEILL, CARE OF THIS NEWSPAPER."

Seventeen

HENRY sat down.

Questions were darting about in his head like birds in a net. He had to wait until they quieted down before he could sort them out.

Why was Kevin looking for Shana and the others? Didn't he know they were in the copper mine? Was he still looking for them? Was he still to be found "care of this newspaper"? Which newspaper?

The piece of paper with the announcement on it was light brown. It crumbled at the edges when he straightened it out. Jane said the island people had left their homes about twenty years ago, so it must be at least that old. But they might have collected the shells and wrapped them away in the basket long before that.

Henry smoothed out one of the other pieces to see if he could find a date or the name of the newspaper on it. There were a lot of figures on one side but they all seemed to be about how much cows weighed. He turned it over and read the printing on the other side.

"Mr. O'Mahoney said in court that the horse and cart were in the middle of the road. . . ."

If Henry had seen those words in a paper at home they might have been some help to him. He could have asked his father how long it had been since there were horses and carts on the roads. But there were horses and carts everywhere around here. He was always passing them on his bicycle.

He heard whistling outside. Jane was coming back. He put the piece of paper with Kevin's announcement on it and the other pieces he had taken off the shells away in his shirt pocket. He wished he could unwrap all the other shells and take those bits of paper too.

Jane's feet made a hollow sound on the wooden stairs. She came into the room. She saw the basket.

"What did you find?"

"Just some old shells."

Jane picked up one of them. She started to pull the paper off it.

"Don't." It was worse than watching someone tear up a letter from home before he had read it. Henry took the shell and unwrapped it for her. It was an oyster shell. Jane dropped it back in the basket. Henry hid the torn piece of paper away in his pocket.

"We'd better go." Jane started for the door. "The wind's dropping."

"Let's take these with us." Henry picked up the basket.

"What do you want them for?"

"I'm interested in . . . shells." He couldn't tell her any more than that without telling her everything.

It was easier going back. The wind was blowing over their left shoulders. The jib stayed on the right side of the mast all the way. Henry kept looking at the basket of shells on the bottom of the boat behind him. He could hardly wait to get home and unwrap every one of them.

His bicycle was on the dock. He hung the basket over the handlebars. He started to thank Jane for the picnic.

"Grandfather's expecting you for dinner."

"Oh." Henry couldn't think of anything else to say.

"Come on."

"I can't. I'm sorry." The unexpected thing was that Henry was sorry. As he bicycled off he felt a little the way he had at Kennedy Airport. He kept wanting to look back, to have one last sight of Jane.

He pedaled as fast as he could along the unpaved road. He didn't see the man until he almost ran into him.

"Hey." He was suddenly there in front of Henry, holding up his hand. "Hey, stop."

Henry squeezed on his brakes. The bicycle slipped sideways under him. He couldn't keep hold of the handlebars. The basket jumped off them. It fell on its side, scattering shells all over the road.

"You ought to look where you're going, kid." The man was holding Henry by the shoulders.

He was a tall man. He had heavy eyebrows and a long face with bulges in it. Henry noticed those things about him after a moment.

The first thing he noticed was that the man was wearing army clothes and a helmet.

Eighteen

"YOU live around here, kid?"

Henry didn't answer. As soon as the man let go of his shoulders all he could think of was finding every one of those shells. If he lost one it was sure to be wrapped in the one piece of newspaper with a helpful clue on it. He picked up the basket and bent over the road collecting them.

"You speak English?"

Henry nodded. Some of the shells had fallen into the ditch.

"Then why don't you answer? You live around here?"

Henry shook his head. It seemed the obvious thing to do to lie to this man. He was like the guard who looked after the gym at school. He acted as though he wanted you to lie to him so he could make trouble for you.

He wasn't a soldier, Henry could see now. There were no badges on his shirt. It wasn't an army helmet he was wearing. There was a flashlight fixed to it. It was none of his business where Henry lived.

"For Pete's sake will you leave those things alone and listen for a moment."

Henry hadn't heard anyone say "for Pete's sake" for weeks. The man was an American. It didn't make Henry feel any friendlier. It only reminded him all the more of the guard at school.

He stretched out on the grass and passed his hand carefully over the bottom of the ditch. His fingers touched one of the shells.

Henry sat up with a jolt. The man was holding him by both elbows. It hurt.

"Are you going to answer me, kid?"

Henry didn't say, "Let go." He thought of something better than that.

"Shuh-I-will-shuh," he said quickly, running the words together the way Mrs. Regan did. "Only-I'm-after-finding-my-messages." Messages was a favorite word of Mrs. Regan's. It meant anything from a letter to a pound of tea.

"Whatever you say, kid." The man let go of him. He seemed suddenly tired. "Isn't there anyone around here who speaks English?" he asked, looking up at the sky.

Henry found the shell in the ditch and put it in his basket. He was almost sure he had them all now. He stood up.

"Can you understand me, kid?"

"Shuh-I-can-shuh." Henry kept his head down, searching the road in case he had missed any.

"Do you know a dame called Fallon?"

"Who-is-it-so?" There was one more over by the hedge. Henry went after it.

"FALLON!"

"I don't." Henry picked up his bicycle. The man didn't try to stop him. Henry hung the basket back on the handlebars. He pushed the bicycle a few yards and then jumped onto it and rode away.

He forgot all about the man as soon as he was safely around the first corner.

He didn't wonder why an American in a miner's helmet was looking for Penelope.

Nineteen

" 'POOR fox,' remarked Resident Magistrate, Mr. S. Large, in District Court yesterday, when Mr. J. O'Keeffe in defence of his client informed the Magistrate that he was only burning a few gorse bushes in order to smoke out a fox. . . ."

Henry put the piece of newspaper with the others. He hadn't found anything that told him which newspaper it was or when Kevin had put in the announcement about Shana and the Sullivans. While he was reading about cattle sales and advertisements for cough syrup, he had gone over the whole story of Kevin and the others.

Kevin rescued the Sullivans from the soldiers. They all hid in the copper mine. They lived on mushrooms at first. Then Kevin discovered how to think up other things. He made them comfortable down there with their own cottage, land, water, food, almost anything they wanted. One day Kevin climbed out of the mine to see if it was safe for them all to come back into the outside world. He never returned.

Shana and the Sullivans thought he had only been gone a few weeks. Henry knew for sure now that they were wrong. Kevin had left the mine at least twenty years ago because the scrap of newspaper he had found on the island was at least twenty years old.

Why had Kevin put in that announcement? If he was looking for Shana and the Sullivans why hadn't he gone back to the mine where he had left them?

There were only three more shells left to unwrap. Three more pieces of newspaper left to look at. The rest were spread out all over Henry's bed.

Eeny-meeny-miny-mo. Henry picked up one of the three shells. He was used to the crumbly paper by now. He managed to smooth it out without losing any of it. It was already torn in an uneven way down the sides. The right-hand column of print had all the last words missing. Most of it was about selling houses. "Disposal of Property," the newspaper called it.

Henry saw the name at once at the bottom.

It was in big letters with a line underneath it.

KEVIN O'NEI

There were only four more half sentences below that.

> Mr. Kevin O'Neill di
> home near Skibbereen last We
> Mr. O'Neill, who lived for m
> America, came back to Ire

Henry found a piece of paper and a pencil. He tried to fill in the missing words.

> Mr. Kevin O'Neill disposed of his
> home near Skibbereen last Wednesday.
> Mr. O'Neill, who lived for many years in
> America, came back to Ireland . . .

That was the best he could do. It wasn't much. But it gave Henry an idea.

He couldn't understand why he hadn't thought of it before.

He started putting the shells back into the basket. He didn't bother to unwrap the last two. He didn't need to.

Henry knew how to find Kevin.

Twenty

HENRY didn't wait to have breakfast the next morning. He took a piece of bread and butter to eat on the way and hurried up to the chimney.

He started to kick the white stone in the usual signal to Shana.

Kick. He counted to twenty-eight.

Kick.

Henry stopped. Someone was watching him from the doorway of one of the tumbledown cottages across the road. A man was standing there, swinging a hammer in his hand the way Henry had seen policemen swing their clubs.

"Hello, kid."

He was wearing the same army pants and shirt and the same miner's helmet with a flashlight on it.

Henry leant against the chimney. There was nothing else he could do so long as the man kept watching him. If the man saw him crawl into the mine he wouldn't go on standing there. He would start asking questions. He might even follow him. He was that sort of person.

He was still swinging his hammer, twirling it, catching it by the handle. Henry couldn't see his eyes but he knew the man was still looking at him. There was no one else to look at.   ·

Henry put his hands in his pockets. He began to

sidle around the chimney. After a dozen steps he was out of sight of the cottages. He paused and waited.

There was the sound of boots crossing the road. Henry still waited. The boot sounds reached the other side of the chimney. They started around it. So did Henry. He walked at the same speed as the boots, keeping the chimney between them. When the boots paused, Henry did too. When the boots walked on, Henry walked on. The only difference between their movements was that Henry didn't make a sound. As far as the man could see or hear, there was no one there.

They both walked clear around the chimney four times before the man decided Henry must have gone off somewhere else. Down the hill. Or behind some gorse bushes. Henry heard him say, "For Pete's sake," several times. The sound of his breathing and his boots grew fainter. He was walking down the hill, stopping now and then to look into the gorse.

Henry finished the signal. The white stone swung back. He crawled through the hole.

"Close the door," he whispered down to Shana as soon as he had hold of the iron ladder. He heard the stone move back into place behind him.

"Did anyone see you?" Shana was waiting in the circle of candles below. She looked frightened.

"No. It's all right." Henry thought of all the things he had to tell her. "Let's go somewhere and sit down," he suggested.

"Did you find Kevin?" Shana led the way down one of the passages with a candle.

"Not yet." They were in a small cave with rough green walls and a low roof.

"Could we have some chairs?" Henry asked.

Shana closed her eyes for a second. It always amazed Henry the way things appeared when she thought of them. They weren't there all at once, the way things are suddenly there in a room when you switch on the light. It was more like the sun coming up in the morning. First there were dark shapes. You could hardly make out what they were. Then as the sun got higher you could see them more and more clearly until it was daylight and everything was complete.

Shana had thought he would like a rocking chair. Henry sat down in it. She put the candle on a stone and sat on the ground. She hadn't thought of a chair for herself, but after a moment Henry could see she had a cushion under her.

He rocked back and forth a couple of times. He wasn't going to tell Shana about Kevin's announcement. It would only worry her if she heard Kevin didn't know where she was.

"I haven't found Kevin yet," he began. "But I know where he was. Maybe not too long ago. He had a home near Skibbereen."

"He sold it." Shana nodded. "He sold it to help people when they had nothing to eat."

"I think he bought another house later . . ." Henry had to be careful what he said. "He went to America for a while after he left you. I expect he was trying to see if he could get you all over there. Then he came back to Ireland . . ."

"Why didn't he come and fetch us?"

It was the question Henry had hoped she wouldn't ask. He decided to tell her the truth.

"I don't know."

"Perhaps the soldiers are watching him."

Henry let that pass. It was as good as anything he could think of.

"Is Kevin still there?" Shana asked.

Henry didn't know that either.

"Then how can we find him?"

Henry rocked again for a moment.

"I know Kevin O'Neill was at his home near Skibbereen," he said slowly, "about . . . well, not all that long ago. And my idea was that you and Johnchristopher and Hester and Martin . . . I'll come with you if you like . . . You see, you could *think* we were all at Kevin's house . . ."

Henry rocked again. When? How long ago? Twenty years? Twenty-five? Thirty? Shana thought Kevin had only left the mine last month. He mustn't talk about time, about years to her.

"The last time Kevin was there," Henry said.

Twenty-one

IT was dark. Dark as midnight without clocks when you wake up in a strange room.

It was cold too. Henry shivered. It must be winter, he decided. He was still holding Shana's hands as he had been holding them in the mine a moment before.

A moment before?

Of course it wasn't. It was one morning in the future when Shana had clasped his hands and closed her eyes, while Johnchristopher and Hester and Martin, suddenly afraid to go with them, tried to smile and gave them messages for Kevin.

Now he and Shana were back in some winter's night that was all over long before Henry walked up to the mine and saw the man in the miner's helmet there. Before he went to Ireland. A night that had passed before Henry was even born.

He was slowly beginning to come back to himself. It was too dark to see, but he could feel his body all the way down to his feet. He could hear the wind straining the branches of a tree over his head. From the smell of the leaves he thought it was probably a cypress.

"Look, over there, the lights," Shana whispered.

Henry had to turn his head to see them. A hundred yards away was the dim mass of a house.

The glow of curtained windows downstairs. A single brighter light above.

"Come on." Henry kept hold of Shana's hand as they walked toward the house.

They were halfway there. The shape of the house was clearer. It was a large rambling place. Henry stopped. He heard men's voices ahead of him in the darkness. He and Shana walked softly forward a few more steps. The voices became sharper. He could hear words.

"They won't be coming now."

"We'll wait here just the same."

"Are you giving us orders?"

"I am."

Henry shivered again. He was only wearing a shirt and jeans, but it wasn't the cold that made him shiver. It was the idea that he was in an unknown time and place listening to voices out of a night long ago.

"Couldn't we wait in the stables then, Sergeant?"

Henry felt Shana's fingers tighten. He guessed the word Sergeant had frightened her.

"All right. All of you, follow me to the stables."

After that there was silence except for the creak of leather, the faint clink of metal. From the sounds Henry felt as though he could see what the men were doing. They were slinging guns over their shoulders. Their footsteps drummed on the hard ground as they moved off.

Shana was pulling at his hand. She dropped to her knees, afraid that if one of the soldiers looked back he might see them in the light from the windows. They waited, crouching side by side, until they couldn't hear the men's steps any longer.

"That's why Kevin hasn't come to fetch us."
There was a strange quaver in Shana's voice. "The
soldiers are watching him."

Henry didn't answer at once. All he could think
of was that somewhere in that house, less than fifty
yards away, was Kevin O'Neill. He remembered the
words he had told Shana to use when she had
thought them here. "The *last* time Kevin was at his
home near Skibbereen." That could mean Kevin
might be leaving any minute. They'd better hurry up
and get to him.

"We'll have to try to slip past the soldiers," he
said.

Shana didn't move.

"It's only the ordinary soldiers who stay outside." There was the same quavering note in her
voice. It wasn't exactly like fear. "The officers always
live in the house when they're watching someone.
They take all the best rooms. That's what they did
last time. Just before the famine. When Kevin refused to drink to the queen."

"The queen?"

"Queen Victoria. They tried to make Kevin drink
to her health. He spat out the wine. Three British
officers came to live in our house. I tried to kill one
of them. They said they'd shoot the cattle if Kevin
didn't send me away. I had to go and stay with Hester. It'll only make trouble for Kevin if they find me
here."

Henry couldn't understand it. It didn't sound
like Shana talking at all. She seemed to have lost all
her usual lively spirit, her confidence in herself.

She might be right about the soldiers though, he
decided. He had no way of knowing what year it was
now. Queen Victoria might still be alive. Things

might not have changed much. There could be British officers in the house who would recognize Shana.

"They don't know *me*," he suggested. "I could try and find Kevin. I could tell him you're here."

"Aren't you afraid?" Shana touched his hand. Her fingers were as hard and cold as bones.

"Sure." Henry was. "But they can't do anything much to me," he said hopefully. "If they catch me, I'll just say I'm American. A friend of Kevin's from New York."

He got to his knees. "You'd better go back to the trees and hide," he told Shana. "I'll try to bring Kevin to you there."

"Thank you." Shana stood up. The next moment she was gone. Henry heard her stumbling footsteps in the darkness as she moved away.

He started toward the house to find Kevin.

Twenty-two

HENRY kept in the shadows.

The first thing to do was to try to find out where the British officers were. The windows on both sides of the front door were curtained. Other lights showed around the corner of the house. He felt the gravel with each foot before putting his weight on it as he walked toward them.

He stepped onto grass. He began to walk more quickly. There were no curtains over these windows. The light from them made long shapes on the lawn. Standing between the shapes Henry could see into a large room.

He couldn't see any soldiers. He stepped closer to the window. Several armchairs, a bearskin rug, a sofa, pictures on the walls, a round table with a lamp on it. Henry looked carefully at the lamp. It had a milky white shade with a glass chimney sticking through it. The top of the chimney was darkened with smoke streaks. They hadn't invented electricity yet.

He leant forward trying to see the rest of the room. There didn't seem to be anybody in it. The long windows were the kind that open like double doors down the middle. Henry pushed against the one he was standing near. It wouldn't open. He started to the next one.

He went back and pressed his face against the glass. There was someone sitting in one of the armchairs.

It wasn't surprising Henry hadn't caught sight of him before. He wasn't very big and he was sitting huddled up between the high arms of the chair with his feet pulled up beside him.

He was wearing a dark jacket with a belt around it and trousers of the same bristly looking cloth. The trousers were tucked into his socks like a baseball player's. He had a thin pointed face and dark hair.

Henry peered in through the next window. He wanted to make sure the boy was alone. He tapped on the glass. He tapped as gently as he could.

The boy in the armchair jumped up as though someone had screamed. He turned and stared at the door.

Henry tapped again. This time the boy realized the sound had come from the window. He walked slowly toward it. He and Henry faced each other through the glass.

It gave Henry a strange feeling. There they were. They seemed to be about the same age. But Henry knew they weren't. The boy was years older than he was. He would be grown-up, he might even be dead before Henry was born.

The boy opened the window. Henry stepped into the room. The boy looked curiously at Henry's clothes. He was particularly interested in his sneakers.

"Are you from the boat?" he asked.

Henry didn't know anything about any boat. He decided not to answer one way or the other. The best thing was to say as little as he could about himself.

"I want to see Kevin O'Neill."

"You can't. You can't do that." The boy looked frightened. "Nobody's allowed to see him."

Henry thought he could guess why not.

"Where are the soldiers?"

"Didn't you see them down at the dock? They were supposed to wait for the boat."

"I heard them." Henry couldn't see any harm in admitting that. "They went off to the stables. Where are the officers?"

The boy didn't seem to understand.

Henry couldn't blame him. If he was sitting at home alone and someone walked in out of the night with a foreign accent and unfamiliar clothes, it would take him a little time to get used to it. The trouble was Henry didn't have much time. Kevin might leave the house forever while they were talking.

"I want to see Kevin O'Neill," he repeated firmly. "I've got to see him."

The boy clasped his hands, lacing the fingers together. He had the same frightened look he had had before when Henry asked for Kevin. It only lasted a moment. He frowned the fear away as though he had made up his mind not to think about it.

"Did you get the guns ashore?" he asked.

It was worse than talking to the boys in the village. The two of them never seemed to be talking about the same thing. Henry had an idea. The piece of newspaper with Kevin's announcement was in his shirt pocket. He showed it to the boy.

"Never mind the guns. It's about this."

The boy looked at the announcement. "Shana?" he asked excitedly. "Do you know where Shana is?"

Henry put the piece of paper back in his pocket. "Let's go," he said. He tried to make it sound like an order.

"All right." The boy walked to the door. Henry stopped him before he opened it.

"Are there any soldiers in the house?"

The boy looked at him suspiciously. "Why are you afraid of the soldiers?"

Henry realized for the first time that he knew nothing about this boy. Seeing him sitting in the armchair he had taken it for granted that he lived here, that he was a friend of Kevin's. It was possible that he was on the other side altogether. He might be the son of one of the British officers who had moved in to watch Kevin.

"I'm not afraid of the soldiers," Henry said cautiously. "I'm only doing what I was told. I was told not to talk to anyone except Kevin."

"Who by?"

"Your friends." Henry thought that sounded safe.

The boy seemed to think so too. "All the soldiers are outside," he said. He opened the door and led the way into the hall.

As he followed the boy up the curving staircase, Henry had the same feeling he had had on the island with Jane. Everything had happened before. He had expected this staircase to be here and to look just like this.

The boy led the way down a long passage. He stopped outside a door at the end. There was a lamp on a bracket beside the door. It made a small hissing sound. The boy's face looked as pale as frost in the wavering light.

"Grandfather's in there," he said.

Twenty-three

HENRY turned the knob and softly opened the door.

He thought at first he had walked into a trap. He was in a small space with a dark wall in front of him. Then he saw that it wasn't a wall he was facing. A folding screen had been set up just inside the door. He had only to step around it to see into the room.

It was the smell that stopped him. He had never smelled anything like it before. There was more than staleness in it. It made Henry think of what Johnchristopher had said about the land, when the potatoes turned black in the fields. It was the smell that comes out of living things when they're rotting.

It held Henry like a net. He stood there behind the screen, trying not to breathe, listening. The unseen room was full of murmurs. A woman's pleading voice saying the same word over and over again. "Father." "Father." A man's gentle warning. "Please, Marguerite. Please."

Another man's gasping breath. A dry rustling in his throat as he strained for air.

And then, breaking through this web of whispers like a knife, Henry heard a single shouted name. "Shana!"

He stepped around the screen. There were three people in the room. A man and a woman were bending over a great highbacked bed. The man had a doctor's listening tube dangling from his neck. The woman was wearing a spreading dress that reached to the floor. She looked about the same age to Henry as his mother. Her sleeves were rolled halfway up her brown arms. She was dark haired and beautiful.

It was the figure between them that held Henry's eyes. Half covered by the tumbled bedclothes, an old man was fighting to raise himself on his elbows. He had white, tangled hair. Except for his eyes his face seemed to be all bone. His fingers tore at the sheets as he strained upright in the bed. He was staring wildly at Henry.

He didn't seem to see him. He didn't seem to see anything. His teeth parted.

"Shana!"

It was a cry of longing and despair. The old man straightened as though a great hand had grasped him. His mouth was an empty darkness. His head fell back on the pillow like a dead weight. The rustling sound from his throat stopped.

Henry shivered. Something seemed to drain out of the old man as he watched him. It was like a broken wave dragging back down the shore, leaving everything cold and still behind it.

Henry understood. He had come to this house on the last night that Kevin would ever spend there.

The night of Kevin O'Neill's death.

Henry never remembered the next minute. He must have run down those familiar stairs, across that familiar hall, and out into the night.

The clouds had broken. Patches of moonlight stained the grass. He recognized the cypress trees at once. Beyond them was the jetty, the stone gate posts.

Shana wasn't by the trees.

He walked on to the dock.

"Shana," he called softly. "Shana."

There was no reply.

"Shana," he called again, more loudly.

"Henry." Her voice was so thin and tired he could scarcely hear it. She was lying like a heap of clothes under the wall of the dock. He took her shoulders, trying to help her to her feet.

"Did you find Kevin?"

"No." He managed to raise her to her knees. "We got here too late. Kevin's gone. He's left."

"Gone where?"

"Shana. Please. Hurry. Stand up. Please. We've got to get back." Henry didn't know how much of the truth he would tell her later. He would think that out later. For the moment he wanted only to get away from this place. Away from this night.

Shana was panting. He could feel the strain in her as she pushed with her hands against the wall behind her and struggled slowly to her feet.

"Give me your hands, Shana. Quick." Henry reached down for them.

Shana was standing upright. She seemed to tower over him. Moonlight whitened her hair. It revealed her face.

It was no longer Shana's face looking down at him. The cheeks were dark hollows. The skin scarred with deep lines.

It was the face of an old woman.

Twenty-four

HENRY didn't try to understand what had happened. He didn't try to figure out why Shana had aged sixty years in the half hour they had been here.

He managed to get hold of the old woman's hands. Her fingers were like bones.

"Quick, Shana," he told her. "Think we're back there. Hurry. Think we're home in the mine."

She closed her wrinkled eyes.

A terrible thought crossed Henry's mind.

"Wait," he shouted.

He hadn't told her when. She had no sense of time. She might think them back there into any day or night in the past hundred years. Climbing out of the chimney, he could find himself living in the days of the famine.

"Think we're back there . . ." But he couldn't tell her the date in which he lived. Even the nineteen hundreds were the distant future to her.

"Think we're back there . . ." he repeated urgently. He could feel that now familiar change in him. His feet, his ankles, his knees were growing out of reach. Instant by instant he was losing all sense of them as they gradually disappeared.

". . . at the time we left."

Only his head remained as he screamed the last word. He closed his eyes.

He opened them.

He was outside the cottage in the great domed cave. Across the field Johnchristopher was digging potatoes. Hester and Martin were collecting them into a sack.

Henry felt Shana's hands in his. Her fingers seemed strong and lively, the skin smooth. He forced himself to look at her face.

The short straight nose, the great dark eyes, the thick black pigtails hanging over her shoulders. Shana looked exactly as she had the first time he saw her. She was a young girl again.

"Shana! Henry!" Johnchristopher and Hester and Martin had seen them. They were running across the field. They gathered close around them.

"Did you find Kevin?"

"Where's Kevin?"

"Where is he?"

Henry had to think before he answered. "Could we go into the cottage?" he said. "Could we go in and sit down?"

Hester brought him a bowl of soup. He was still too shaken and confused to be hungry, but he spooned some of it slowly into his mouth. It gave him a little more time.

They were all leaning toward him as they had the first morning when he told them the story of Tom Sawyer. It had been easier then. He hadn't had to worry about anyone except himself. What he told them now could change their whole lives. It was waiting for Kevin that kept them here. If they knew he was dead, that he was never coming back, they might decide to leave the mine.

Henry knew now what would happen to them if

they did. He had seen what happened to Shana. In a few minutes she had become her real age. The age she had been the night Kevin died. About seventy, Henry guessed. If they climbed out of the mine into the present day, even Martin would suddenly find himself over a hundred years old.

How long could any of them live outside in the present?

"I didn't see Kevin," Henry began. "It was . . . bad luck. I only missed him by a few minutes. He'd only just left the house when I got there."

"Do you know how he is?"

"Did anyone say where he'd gone?"

"Did you talk to anyone at the house?"

"Yes, I did. I talked to Kevin's . . ." Henry stopped himself. He was going to say "talked to Kevin's grandson." He had forgotten they still thought of Kevin as a young man. "To a friend of his," he said instead. "Kevin's fine. I'll keep on trying to find him for you."

"Why hasn't he been to fetch us?"

It was Hester who asked. Henry had known one of them would.

"Because of the soldiers." He was glad to hear Shana answer for him. "There were soldiers all around the house. They're still watching Kevin."

Johnchristopher nodded. "I thought that was why," he said.

"He'll be here as soon as he can slip away," Hester added.

"Traveling by night," Martin explained.

Henry stood up. He thanked Hester for the soup. He wanted to get back to his own room. He wanted to sit there alone and think. He promised to return soon. As soon as he had any more news of Kevin.

Shana showed him the way. They climbed the twisting steps. They passed the cave where the Ulalus lived. Henry heard their deep unpleasant breathing. They paused for a moment in the ring of candles at the bottom of the chimney.

"You will go on trying to help us?" Shana asked.

Henry promised he would. He didn't say how. That was one of the things he wanted to think about alone.

He started up the iron ladder. He was on the top rung, crawling toward the opening in the chimney, when that terrible thought crossed his mind again.

Had Shana heard those last words he had screamed at her on the dock near Kevin's house?

Had she thought them back into the present day?

What kind of world was he going to find outside?

Twenty-five

THERE were no ragged, starving looking people in sight.

The row of cottages was there. They didn't have any roofs on them.

Henry pushed his head out a little farther. The sun was shining. He pulled his head back.

He could hear a ringing metal sound like someone hammering on stone. It came from quite close. A soldier knocking a house down with a pickaxe might make that sort of noise, he thought.

He peered out again.

Ten yards away, on the other side of the chimney, a man was swinging a pick at the ground. Beside him was a box with wires coiling out of it. He was hacking away at the edge of the road as though he hated every inch of it. His anger and violence weren't getting him very far. The blade of the pickaxe bounced off the smooth, half-buried rocks without leaving more than a scratch on them.

He was wearing army clothes, but he wasn't a soldier. It was the American in the miner's helmet.

Henry would never have believed he could be glad to see him. But he was. If the American was still there it must be roughly the same date as the last time he saw him. It was probably the same day.

Henry crawled softly forward out of the gap in

the chimney. The white stone swung into place behind him. The man had his back turned. Henry kept to the long grass on his own side of the road. He was safely past him before the American saw him.

"Hey, kid!"

Henry kept going. He broke into a run. He didn't head for the gate. He took to the fields, darting between the gorse bushes. He knew the ground better than the American did. The man had given up and gone back to his pickaxe long before Henry reached the house.

Mrs. Regan was in the kitchen. She asked Henry if he wanted a bacon sandwich. It was all right. No one had missed him. He could only have been gone a few hours.

He thanked Mrs. Regan and told her he wasn't hungry. He went upstairs to his room. He locked the door and sat down on the bed.

There was the tall chimney. He could see it through the window. Down below it, inside the hill, were the rambling tunnels of the mine, the huge cave with the field and the cottage. And there were Shana and Johnchristopher and Hester and Martin. They might be having night down there now, sleeping safely in the beds they'd thought up. Or perhaps they thought it was dinner time and they were talking around the table. Or Shana and Martin might have thought of a stream and gone swimming.

Whatever they were doing they always seemed happy together.

They would stay there, happy and safe, so long as they had hope. So long as each of their timeless uncounted days brought them the hope of Kevin's return.

Henry remembered the old man fighting for breath in the awful smell of that room.

He remembered the boy, Kevin's grandson, sitting in the chair in the room below. The room with the tall windows. He thought of the hall, the curving staircase. The cypress trees. The dock. He remembered how familiar it had all seemed to him.

Five minutes later Henry unlocked his door. He paused at the top of the stairs. Someone was talking in the living room.

"She's after going to her work." It was Mrs. Regan's voice.

"When do you expect her back?" Henry recognized the other voice too. He had heard it just now, yelling "Hey, kid" after him.

"Only herself could tell you that."

"What?"

The voices grew fainter. They were only sounds now.

Angry, demanding American sounds. Then calm, patient Irish ones. Henry crept down three more stairs.

"For Pete's sake." It was a cry of anguish. Henry peered between the banisters.

The American was bending over the wastepaper basket beside the kitchen door. "She never even *opened* them." He was holding several letters. Henry recognized the envelopes from the Bonoco Co., Inc., Urgent.

Mrs. Regan said something calm from the kitchen.

"What?" The American followed her inside.

Henry's bicycle was on the porch. He got it to the gate without hearing anyone shouting after him.

He jumped on and pedaled off along the coast road.

He knew why Kevin's house had seemed so familiar to him.

He was going there now to see Jane and The Lieutenant.

Twenty-six

"PLEASE get in touch with Mr. Kevin O'Neill care of this newspaper," The Lieutenant read aloud. He was sitting in his usual chair with the high sides. Henry and Jane were on the sofa.

Henry could see the room had changed. It looked bigger. Perhaps someone had built onto it at some time, or a dividing wall had been knocked down. The curtains and the chair covers were different. The round table was gone. There were electric lights instead of oil lamps.

But he had guessed right. There was the window he had tapped on. This was the room in which he had talked to the boy.

The Lieutenant held the piece of newspaper in his hands, looking at it with a sad half smile.

"My grandfather ran that announcement in the *Skibbereen Eagle* for over twenty years," he said. "After he came back to Ireland he had them print it every week until he died."

"My grandfather,"—the boy had called Kevin O'Neill that too. It scared Henry a little to think what that meant. It seemed to him only a few minutes since he had come here the night of Kevin's death. But he was sure it was the same boy sitting in that same chair. Except that now the boy was an old man.

"Didn't he remember . . ." Henry had to be

careful not to give Shana and the Sullivans away. He had to pretend he didn't know anything about them. "Didn't he remember the last time he had seen his . . . the friends he was trying to find?"

"He lost touch with his sister during the famine."

"His sister?" Henry was only pretending not to understand.

"Shana. Shana O'Neill. She must have been a wild little girl. She tried to shoot a British officer who was billeted in their house. Kevin had to send her to live with the Sullivans for a while. Then the potato crop failed. My grandfather . . ." The Lieutenant's eyes brightened with pride. "He was always a strong rebel. He got into some kind of trouble himself."

He stole a sheep, Henry could have told him. He gave it to the Sullivans.

"He had to go on the run," The Lieutenant went on. "And then somehow or other he managed to escape to America."

"On a coffin ship," Jane said. Henry could see she had heard the story before. She still seemed excited by it.

"That's what they called them," The Lieutenant explained. "It was the right name for them too. Hundreds of poor creatures shut up in the hold without medicines or even fresh water. On some of those coffin ships half the passengers died before they reached the New World."

"Famine fever," Jane said.

"Typhus." The Lieutenant nodded. "Typhus followed the famine in Ireland. My grandfather almost died of it. When he came back to life he found himself in a quarantine camp on Grosse Isle near Quebec. He didn't know how he had got there. He couldn't remember anything of the voyage. Or even getting on the ship."

"So that's why he couldn't remember where he'd left Shana," Henry said. Or even being in the copper mine, he thought.

"The last thing he remembered was going on the run," The Lieutenant told him. "And that was quite early in the famine. Almost two years before. He thought Shana and the Sullivans might have come over on the same coffin ship with him. He searched all over Quebec and Montreal for them, for anyone who might have seen them."

"Alive or dead," Jane put in.

"He refused to believe they were dead. It was a kind of faith with him. He was sure they were alive. He was sure they were safe somewhere. He wanted to work his way back to Ireland to find them. But then he heard in Montreal that many of his friends here had been arrested and the British were still after him. So he went on to the United States."

"He joined the Niners," Jane added proudly. "And went out West."

"The Forty-niners?" Henry asked. He had learnt about them at school. Sutter's Mill and San Francisco, and the wagons crossing the mountains to California, and the gold rush.

"I know it was something to do with nine," Jane agreed. "He had all sorts of adventures after that. He was captured by Indians. But he made friends with them. He lived with them for years."

"That's how he met my grandmother." The Lieutenant smiled. "She was Indian. They got themselves some land out in Colorado later and did very well.

My mother was born there. But my grandfather, Kevin, could never rid himself of the idea that Shana was still alive, waiting for him somewhere. He came back here after my grandmother died. He bought this house and settled here. He was over sixty by then and Shana would have been a middle-aged woman herself—if she was still alive. But he wouldn't give up. He kept looking for her, trying to trace her. He kept running the same announcement every week, hoping someone would come forward with news of her."

The Lieutenant clasped his hands in his lap, lacing the fingers together. He did it exactly the way the boy had. There was a silence.

"When did Kevin O'Neill die?" Henry asked.

"Over sixty years ago. The winter of Nineteen Hundred and Eight." The Lieutenant unclasped his hands and settled back in his chair. "I'll never forget that night. My father was away. In Dublin, I think. My mother and the doctor were upstairs with Grandfather. He'd been ill for several weeks. I wanted to go up to see him. My mother wouldn't let me. She wouldn't let anyone into the room. I sat down here. I sat here the whole night. Waiting. Waiting to be told he was dead."

He stopped speaking. He was looking toward the windows.

Henry looked at them too.

"There were soldiers out there," The Lieutenant went on. "I could hear their voices and the stamping of their feet. They were all around the house that night."

"English soldiers?"

"God, no. Irish. My grandfather's own men. He

was the commander of the rebel forces in the district. They were expecting a cargo of guns to be landed at the dock here. They were out there waiting for a signal from the boat. It never came. It was a cold, wild night."

Henry remembered the voices he had heard. "They'll never be coming now." The sound of the men marching off to the stables. Shana had been frightened and had gone down to the dock. And then he had come here to this room.

There was a question he knew he had to ask. He was afraid of hearing the answer to it. But he had to know.

"Did anyone come here that night?"

The Lieutenant picked up Kevin's announcement. He looked at it. He looked at Henry.

"It's strange," he said. "I was thinking about that this morning. Someone did come here. He came to those windows. He was only a boy. About my own age. I thought he was from the boat."

The old man moved his hand as though trying to hold on to something.

"It's all so long ago," he said softly. "I can't remember what he looked like. What we talked about. Where he went. But the strange thing is that's the first time I've ever remembered him at all. Just now. This morning. It suddenly came to my mind. The boy tapping on the window. Walking into this room."

Henry didn't say anything. The same words were sounding over and over again in his head. Johnchristopher's words.

"We must never change anything outside."

Henry had changed one thing now. By coming here on the night of Kevin's death he had changed

The Lieutenant's memory of it. He had added something to the old man's mind that had never been there before. The memory of that boy—himself.

It gave Henry an uneasy feeling of power.

It frightened him.

Twenty-seven

"I TOLD him you were after going to work," Mrs. Regan was saying as Henry left his bicycle on the porch. He walked into the living room.

"Who was he?" Penelope was sitting on the sofa with her elbows on her knees. There was white dust all over her sweater. She looked tired.

"He said his name was . . ." Mrs. Regan glanced at the back of her hand. She often wrote things there. Things she wanted to remember like "Three milk" or "Take laundry." She found the man's name.

"Mr. Fowler," she told Penelope.

"I don't know any Flowers."

"He sent you letters, he said."

"I never got them."

"They're in the trash there, so." Mrs. Regan pointed to the wastepaper basket by the door.

Penelope didn't get up or even turn to look. She was rubbing her forehead.

"I don't see how anybody could be expected to work with people calling them up and writing them letters all the time," she said. "If that man Flower ever comes here again, tell him I've left, Mrs. Regan. Tell him I'm dead. Tell him anything you like. I'm not going to talk to him. Ever."

"I'll tell him you're after going for a holiday."

Mrs. Regan started to take off her apron. Henry walked over to her. He knew it was no use trying to say anything to Penelope. She was staring at the carpet in that exhausted, listening way she often did in the evenings.

"I won't be in for dinner," he said. "I'm going back to The Lieutenant's and Jane's. Will you tell Penelope that before you leave, please."

Mrs. Regan said she'd try.

Henry thanked her and hurried out. He wasn't going back to The Lieutenant's. He was going to see Shana and the Sullivans. He was going to see them for the last time.

He had thought it all out. He wasn't going to interfere in things he didn't understand any more. Ever. He had made enough mistakes already. "Mr. Kevin O'Neill di . . ." He should have guessed that "di" was the beginning of "died," not "disposed of." He wasn't going to risk any more mistakes like that. The next time he and Shana tried to think themselves where Kevin was, they might end up in a coffin with a skeleton.

At the same time he couldn't go on lying to Shana and the others. He couldn't climb down into the copper mine every day and go on telling them stories to keep their hope alive.

He was going to say he had to go back to America. Back to the little town on the banks of the Mississippi. He was going to tell them one last big lie about Kevin. He was going to pretend he'd had a message from him. Kevin had had to go on the run again. He hadn't forgotten them. He would never forget them. He would come back to them as soon as he could. As soon as he could slip past the soldiers.

If he did that, Henry hoped, they would stay in the mine. They would never know Kevin was dead. They would go on living their safe, happy, timeless lives.

He knew he would miss Shana. He would miss them all. He hated the thought of saying good-bye to them. That was why he was going to do it now. He was afraid if he waited until tomorrow he might change his mind. He might go on . . .

He didn't know what he might do.

Henry had had enough of the unknown. For the rest of the summer he would swim in the cove. He would bicycle over to The Lieutenant's. He would go sailing with Jane and explore the far islands.

He waited for a moment at the foot of the chimney to get his breath back after climbing the hill. He kicked the white stone in the usual signal. It swung back.

Dropping to the ground, Henry crawled into the hole. He saw the ring of candles below. He stretched out his hand toward the top rung of the iron ladder.

It was just out of reach. He would have to crawl a little farther. He tried to draw up his foot to push himself forward. Something tight and hard was locked around his ankle.

His shirt was bunching under his arms. The iron rung was getting farther and farther out of reach. He was being pulled backward through the gap in the chimney.

He spread his arms wide. His elbows stuck against the rough stones on either side. He just had time to yell into the cave where Shana would be waiting for him.

"Hide," Henry shouted.

He couldn't keep his elbows out any longer. He was dragged back out of the chimney. Grass brushed his face. He managed to raise his head and look behind him.

The American in the miner's helmet was kneeling on the ground there. He was holding Henry firmly by both ankles.

"Hullo, kid," he said. "Going somewhere?"

Twenty-eight

"SHUH you saved my life so," Henry said quickly in his best imitation of Mrs. Regan. "I was just after . . ."

"Cut that out. Stop it." The American let go of his ankles. "You quit that. You hear?" He grabbed Henry by the shoulders and jerked him to his feet.

"I know all about you, kid." He stood up himself, forcing Henry's head back. Henry found himself looking into the angry bulging face under the miner's helmet. "You're American and that crazy Fallon woman's your aunt. So don't give me any more of that Irish double-talk. Right?"

"Right."

The man's bony fingers were hurting his shoulders. But the thing that bothered Henry much more than the pain was that Shana had forgotten to swing the stone back into place. The entrance to the chimney was still wide open. Henry could tell that from the way the American was looking at it over his head. He was smiling.

"What's it like down there, kid?" he asked.

"Ow." Henry pretended he was in too much pain to answer. "Ow."

"Okay." The man loosened his fingers a little. "I'll let you go if you talk sense."

Henry nodded. His shoulders were released.

One of the big hard hands kept a hold on his shirt.

"My name's Fowler," the American went on. "Bob Fowler. Bonoco Co., Inc., of Montana. Ever heard of them?"

"No."

"Copper," Fowler explained. "I've come five thousand miles to look inside that mine. And all I get is a run-around. No speak English. No answer the phone. That Fallon dame doesn't open my letters. I've tried blasting my way in, and I can't even make enough of a dent in that rock to plant a stick of dynamite. But you've been down there, haven't you, kid? You go down there all the time."

"I've never really . . ." Henry stopped. Fowler had a grip on his shoulders again.

"You were down there over an hour this morning. Right?"

"Right."

"Okay." Fowler's hand moved back to Henry's shirt. "What did you find?"

"Nothing." Even if he managed to wriggle free and shout down to Shana to close the stone, Henry knew it wouldn't do any good. Now that Fowler knew the way in, he would blast a hole in the chimney with his dynamite if he had to. "There's nothing down there," he said. "Nothing but a lot of old caves and tunnels."

"Water?"

"No."

Henry saw too late he had said the wrong thing. Fowler was smiling again.

"Great. Then let's go. Let's have a look at those caves. That's what I came for. You first, kid."

Henry was forced down to his knees. He was

half lifted and swung over onto his chest. Two hands gripped his ankles again. A few inches in front of him was the gap in the chimney. He was pushed into it.

The ring of lighted candles was still there. Henry climbed slowly down the iron ladder. Fowler's boots kept knocking his fingers as the American followed him from rung to rung.

"For Pete's sake." They stood inside the ring. Fowler looked at the candles. "Where did those come from?"

"I left them there," Henry told him quickly. "When I was down here before."

He couldn't tell whether Fowler believed him or not. The American switched on the flashlight on his helmet. Turning his head slowly he shone the beam of light over the walls of the cave. He whistled.

"Green," he said. "Green as my valley. If the rest of it's anything like this, Bonoco's got a fortune here."

"How?" Henry could guess most of the answer. "What are they going to do?"

"Buy it and strip it." Fowler's hammer was swinging from his wrist by its strap. He walked over to the wall and hacked off a small piece of rock. "We'll tear this place wide open and bull out every ounce of copper." He put the chip of rock in his pocket. "Let's have a look at the rest of it."

Henry had never learned his way alone down the twisting tunnels to the enormous cave and the Sullivans' cottage. He tried to figure out now which way it wasn't. It was bad enough that Fowler and his company were planning to tear the whole copper mine apart. There would be time to worry about that later. For the moment Henry gave his whole mind to worrying about how to keep Fowler from finding Shana and the others. He would never leave them alone once he found them. He wasn't the kind to leave anything as he found it.

Henry was sure that each time Shana had led him to the cottage from here, she had started off to the right of the iron ladder. He chose the tunnel going in the opposite direction. He walked slowly into it.

The beam of the flashlight shone over his shoulder. It lit the way as Fowler followed a step behind him.

The tunnel turned and twisted. It went downhill and then climbed again. At times the roof was so low that Henry had to crawl on his hands and knees. Now and then Fowler would tell him to stop while he hacked away another chip of rock. Each time Henry stopped without being told to, he felt Fowler's hand pushing him forward.

Henry thought about trying to escape. He could suddenly run for it into one of the side tunnels. But Fowler on his own was an even greater danger. He was more likely to find the Sullivans' cottage alone than he was with Henry trying to lead him away from it. Besides, Fowler had the only light.

It shone on the bark of a tree in front of Henry. On the wet face of a rock. It was like looking at pictures one after the other as the beam lit them up. There was something familiar about the pictures to Henry. He had a sudden sick feeling this was the way he had come with Shana.

He felt wood under his feet. He was crossing a footbridge.

A few more yards and he would reach the top of

the cliff, the twisting steps going down into the field. He looked desperately for a turning off from the tunnel. He reached the mouth of a cave.

Henry stopped. A horrible idea had slid into his mind. He tried to push it away. It kept creeping back.

He recognized the opening to the cave. From beyond it came a familiar sound. A sound that could mean safety to Shana and the Sullivans.

It was the deep, unpleasant breathing of the Ulalus.

Twenty-nine

"GO ahead, kid."

It was the most difficult decision Henry had ever had to make.

Straight ahead was the cliff, the Sullivans' cottage. There would be no more safety for Shana and the others if he took that way. Fowler would drag them all out into the open. Into the present. Henry remembered Shana's withered face on the dock near Kevin's house. She was twice as old as that now.

To the right, inside the cave, were the Ulalus. "Enormous black wolves. As big as horses."

Henry had never liked Fowler. He never would like him. He wondered if there was anyone in the world who would really miss him.

But . . . still! Henry could imagine those enormous black wolves, their lolling tongues, the long white teeth.

"Go ahead, kid."

It was the feel of Fowler's hand on his shoulder that decided Henry. Fowler would dig his hard fingers into Shana's shoulder too as he dragged her out into the present.

He took a step toward the cave. The breathing sound grew louder. He let his left leg go limp. He stumbled and fell.

"Ohhh," Henry moaned, lying on the ground. "Ohhh."

"What's the matter?" There was no sympathy in Fowler's voice. He sounded annoyed.

"My ankle." Henry rubbed it. "I've twisted my ankle."

"Can't you get up?"

"I don't know." Henry pretended to try. He decided to give Fowler one last chance. "I guess I could just manage to hobble back to the chimney," he said.

Fowler didn't answer. He turned his head so that the light on his helmet shone into the cave. The beam carried for a few yards and then was lost in the deep blackness.

"What's in there?" he asked.

"My ankle. Can't we go back to the chimney?"

But Fowler didn't want to go back to the chimney. He wanted to see the rest of the mine first. He wanted to hack away some more chips of rock. He wanted to be able to tell the Bonoco Co., Inc., just how much of a fortune there was for them here.

He took three steps forward into the cave. He paused, listening.

"What's that noise?"

There was still time to save Fowler at that moment. Henry could never forget that later. He had only to tell Fowler something like the truth. "Wild animals." He only had to give him the slightest warning.

Fowler was swinging the hammer dangling from his wrist, catching it by the handle, twirling it like a policeman's club.

"It's a waterfall," Henry told him.

118

Fowler nodded. He was swinging and twirling and catching his hammer as he walked on into the cave.

There are some sounds you hear only once in your life that you never forget. Henry had been in a store with his mother one afternoon when two cars collided head-on outside. He still woke at night sometimes to the scream of tires, the tearing clangor of metal.

But those sounds were like music compared to the ones he heard now.

Fowler's screams were not the worst part of them. They ended quite soon.

It wasn't the greedy slavering of the Ulalus that was the worst part either. That was in the background.

The worst sound by far was the brittle crunching of bones.

Thirty

HENRY scrambled to his feet. He pressed his hands to his ears. He fled.

There were no lights burning in the Sullivans' cottage. It looked like late evening in the enormous cave. Henry could barely see his way as he hurried down the twisting steps.

P-o-o-o-m!

It sounded like an explosion. The echo of it seemed to go on and on around the great domed roof. Henry darted behind a rock. There was another echoing p-o-o-o-m. A stone leapt into the air a few yards away from him. Someone was shooting at him from the field below.

"It's me," Henry shouted. "It's all right. I'm alone." He had never felt so much alone in his life.

There was no answer from below. He waited behind the rock. There was no more shooting. He put his head out. Nothing happened. He felt his way down the steps.

He found Martin halfway across the field. He was lying face down in the grass with one end of a huge long-barreled gun pressed against his shoulder. He kept the other end pointing at Henry.

"Who goes there?" he asked.

"It's me. Henry."

"Who else?"

"Nobody."

"Are you really alone, Henry?" Martin stood up, holding the gun like a battle standard. It was a lot taller than he was. "Shana said you'd been captured." Martin peered past him into the twilight. "What happened to the soldiers?"

"I lost him." Henry didn't want to talk about that yet. The sound of those crunching bones was still too close. "Where's Shana?" he asked.

Before Martin could tell him, the lights went on in the cottage. Shana and the Sullivans were running toward him.

All Henry's plans to say good-bye to them were forgotten at once. They were so glad to see him. As they gathered around him, smiling and repeating his name, they seemed to him the only friends he had in the world. The only people who could help him now.

Because everything was changed now. Henry couldn't put off thinking about it any longer. He had murdered Fowler. He could tell himself it wasn't really his fault. But he didn't believe it.

He had wanted Fowler to walk into that cave. And he had.

He had wanted the Ulalus to eat him. And they did.

Perhaps if Henry had had time to sit down and think, he might not have done what he did next. He didn't give himself time. He didn't want to sit down. He didn't want to think. He was too busy wanting to run away.

Shana and the Sullivans could help him do that better than anyone he had ever known. They could help him run five thousand miles in an instant. Not only five thousand miles, but so far away in time no one would ever be able to find him again.

"We've all got to get out of here. Quick!" Henry said. He took Shana's hands. He tried for a moment to tell her what to think.

Before he could find the right words he saw an easier way to do it.

"Think I can take you to Kevin," he said. "All of you join hands and think I can do it."

His own fear must have frightened them. They obeyed him at once. Martin put down his gun. Henry made sure they were all linked together, hand in hand, in a ring. He closed his eyes.

"We're all where Kevin was," he thought slowly and clearly.

Where? How long ago?

They didn't want to find themselves in the middle of a gun fight with Indians.

"Just *before* he started West," Henry finished.

He wondered desperately if he had left anything out. He was already beginning to lose all feeling in his toes.

"Back in Eighteen Forty-nine," Henry added quickly.

Thirty-one

MUD.

That was the first thing Henry saw when he opened his eyes. He couldn't see his feet. He was standing up to his ankles in mud.

Shana and the Sullivans were too. Henry was still holding Shana's hand on one side and Martin's on the other. He looked around to see where he was.

He had expected to find himself in a town. The kind of town Tom Sawyer lived in. A school. A church. Long whitewashed fences.

There wasn't a building in sight. He was in a field. It was the biggest field he had ever seen. It seemed to go on forever. There were no trees, no hedges. There was nothing but land all the way to the horizon.

"Where are we, Henry?" Shana tugged at his hand. He let go of her so that he could keep his balance while he got one foot loose from the mud. When he put it down again he was facing her.

At first all he could think was that her clothes had shrunk. Her dress was tight across her shoulders and under her arms. Her wrists strained out of the sleeves. Then he realized that, like that night at Kevin's house, he was looking up into her face. She had grown at least two inches since she had left the copper mine.

Martin had too. He could hardly move in his jacket, and there was a long stretch of leg between the top of his socks and the bottom of his trousers.

He should have expected it, Henry told himself. He should have remembered that by 1849 Shana and the Sullivans were all about two years older than they usually thought they were. He wished he'd had the sense to think something about that, about a change of clothes for them, before he'd brought them here.

He was glad to see that Johnchristopher and Hester had changed less than the others. The lines Johnchristopher had made at the corners of his eyes by smiling were a little deeper and Hester's hair grayer. But, being grown up already, they hadn't got any bigger. Their clothes still fitted them.

"Where are we, Henry?" Shana asked again.

"We're in America," Henry told them all. "I'm not exactly sure where. But with any luck . . ."

It struck him that the words he had thought to get them here had been much too vague. *"We're all where Kevin was before he started West."* Why hadn't he at least said, "Where Kevin *is*"?

"With any luck," Henry repeated, "Kevin's around here somewhere, not too far away."

Kevin. The name had its usual magical effect on them. They all brightened at once. The first thing, Hester said, was to get out of this mud.

Henry could see now that they were standing in the middle of a wide rutted track that stretched straight away across the plain in both directions. Beside the track the ground looked firmer. The earth was spotted with tufts of grass and small thorny bushes. Pulling their feet clear, step by step, they all struggled to the nearest patch of dry ground.

"My feet." Martin was trying to pull his boots off. They looked as though they had been dipped in melted chocolate. He had to claw the mud away to find the laces. Shana took her shoes off too.

"Put them back on," Hester told them both. "You can't walk about in your socks with all these thorns in the ground."

"I can't get them back on," Martin complained.

"They're too small for me," Shana added.

Hester knelt down and looked at Martin's boots. She moved over to Shana.

"Your feet have swollen. Both of you." She sounded puzzled.

Henry wasn't puzzled. Their feet hadn't swollen. They'd grown like the rest of them. He felt it was time they all sat down and had a long think about what to do next. He told Hester so.

They found a patch of ground that had been cleared of thorns. Nearby, Henry could see a circle of scorched earth. Someone had camped here not too long ago, he thought.

Kevin?

Was that why they had found themselves in this place? Had Kevin stopped here for the night on his way down from Canada "before he started West"?

Shana and the Sullivans were sitting facing him. As usual when they were waiting for him to tell them something, he couldn't decide where to begin.

The one place not to begin, he saw, was at the beginning. There was no sense in telling them they were all two years older. It would only lead to a lot of questions. "Why haven't you grown too?" was the first one he could think of. He didn't know that himself. The truth was—now he thought about it—he had no right to be here at all. Back in 1849 he hadn't been born yet. His great-grandfather probably hadn't been born yet. But here he was, still Henry, still comfortably wearing his usual clothes and feeling the same as he always did.

"We've come a long way," he said at last. "A long way from Ireland. Maybe five thousand miles. And I guess we've all changed a bit on the journey." He stopped to see if they would accept that.

Hester nodded. "I do feel a little tired," she said. Johnchristopher admitted that he did too.

"The point is," Henry went on quickly, "that Kevin's around here somewhere, not too far away. At least he was here, not too long ago. And the point is we've got to find him." He didn't pause this time. Hester nodded again. "So there's nothing to worry about. Really. All we've got to do is to think of all the things we need right away, before we start out to look for him. New shoes for Shana and Martin first. Food and water." He looked up at the sky. The sun was shining, but it wasn't very bright or very high. He was already getting cold in his denim shirt and jeans. "And some warm clothes for all of us," he added.

"That's a good idea, Henry." Johnchristopher smiled.

"We all need some new shoes," Hester agreed, looking at Henry's sneakers. "Good strong boots." She took Shana's and Martin's hands. Henry reached out to Johnchristopher. They completed the ring.

They closed their eyes.

The first thing Henry saw when he opened his

eyes this time was his own denim shirt. Then his faded jeans. Then his mud-covered sneakers. He looked at Shana. She was still wearing the same tight dress. The same cotton socks.

Martin picked up his boots and tried to push his feet into them. They were still too small for him.

They could no longer think up all the things they needed.

They had lost that gift when they left the copper mine.

Thirty-two

HESTER recovered first.

"Never mind," she said. "We'll manage somehow until we find Kevin."

Henry wasn't so sure. Here they were, in the middle of nothing. He had never seen such an empty, hopeless place in his life. There was no shade. No shelter. No sign of life to head for. Nothing.

They had nothing themselves either. Nothing to eat or drink. No matches to light a fire when night came. No blankets. Shana and Martin didn't even have any shoes.

It was all his fault.

He had been so frightened by what had happened to Fowler—by the feeling *that* was all his fault too—he hadn't taken the time to sit down and think things out.

At least he was sitting down now. The first thing to think about was shoes. Henry took off his sneakers and handed them to Shana.

"Try these on," he suggested. "And, Martin, you can try Shana's shoes on."

Hester and Johnchristopher got the idea at once. Martin's boots were too small for any of them, but that still left four pairs of shoes between five people.

For the next few minutes they were all busy

passing and trying on shoes. It didn't work out as well as Henry had hoped. Martin could wear Shana's shoes, but Shana couldn't wear Henry's sneakers. She could only wear Hester's boots. That meant three of them would have to take turns going barefoot. Johnchristopher insisted on being the first. Hester tore some strips off her underskirt and bandaged his feet with them. They were ready to start.

"Which way, Henry?"

It was Hester who asked, but they were all waiting for his answer.

Henry looked up at the sky. It seemed to him the sun had dropped a little. It could only have dropped toward the west. West was the way Kevin was heading. Henry pointed toward the sun.

They walked for an hour. They didn't see anything. Worse than that, nothing changed. It was like being at sea without islands or coastlines. There was no way of telling from anything around them that they were moving at all.

The bandages kept shifting on Johnchristopher's feet. He had to stop and retie them. Henry saw bloodstains on the strips of cloth.

Soon it would be Hester's turn to walk without shoes. And after that, Shana's.

Still no one complained. No one blamed Henry. They only spoke once.

"It was worse during the famine," Hester said.

"It was colder," Martin agreed.

"And we had to beg," Johnchristopher added.

After an hour they stopped and rested. Hester gave Johnchristopher his boots back. It took him a long time to get them on over his bruised, cut feet.

Henry wandered off a little way by himself. If he

could climb a tree, he thought, he might be able to see something. There were no trees to climb. He looked up at the sky. The sun was closer to the rim of the land. Henry could feel how cold the night was going to be. A thin black cloud trailed across the sun. He watched it, waiting for it to pass. He could see it moving, but there was always more of it. It kept straggling up from the land.

Henry ran back to the others. He was shouting before he reached them.

"Smoke! Smoke!" He pointed at the sun as he came to a stop. "I can see smoke. Look. Over there."

They were all standing up. They looked to the west.

"Camp fires," Henry said. "There are people ahead. There's got to be."

Thirty-three

IT was dark before they had gone much farther.

As soon as the sun touched the land it seemed to slip out of sight in a second. For a little while it left a fading glow in the sky. Then it was night.

At least there was no danger of losing their way. They could see the pinpoint lights of the fires ahead. How far away were they? Henry wondered. How far could you see across a dead flat plain? Twenty miles?

No matter how far it was, they had to go on. It was too cold to stop. It was too cold to rest for a moment longer than it took Hester to put on Johnchristopher's boots again. She wouldn't let Shana take her turn going without shoes. It didn't make any sense, she said, for more than two of them to get sore feet.

They kept close together for fear of losing each other. Henry did his best to lead the way. The moon was too new to be much help. With the glow of the stars it gave just enough light to show up the bigger thorn bushes before he stumbled over them. He had to lift his feet as high as he could with each step to avoid the smaller ones. If he didn't the thorns stung him through the canvas of his sneakers.

He tried to think about the camp fires ahead. He imagined getting there, sitting down. The warmth of the flames. Hot coffee in tin mugs. Great thick bacon sandwiches. The same words kept sounding in his head as though someone else was saying them.

"The fires. The fires of salvation."

After a while they formed a rhyme.

"Those fires are the fires of salvation.

All around them the desert is bare.

We would starve. We would die of starvation,

Except for the sand which is there."

The silly joke made him want to laugh. He wondered if he was going a little crazy. He remembered he was forgetting to lift his feet. It seemed strange he hadn't been stung by thorn bushes.

He couldn't see any thorn bushes.

Henry realized he had wandered back onto the wide rutted track. The new moon was higher in the sky. He could see that the track was even wider here. The ruts were deeper. But along the verge the ground felt firm. Henry knelt to look at it more closely. The others stopped and watched him. The earth was packed down, almost smooth, as though an army had tramped over it.

All the nonsense he had been thinking to forget how cold and tired he was cleared out of his mind. He felt more hopeful. If Kevin had joined the track at the place where they had found themselves, hundreds of others must have joined it at other points along the last few miles. A great flood of them turning west along the same trail. Toward what? Some meeting place? Those camp fires ahead?

Maybe it was going to be all right after all. Maybe they would find Kevin there.

Henry moved on. The going was easier along the edge of the track. He no longer had to pick his way. If he kept his eyes on the ruts beside him, all he had to do was go on putting one foot in front of the other.

Drag one foot forward. Put it down in front of the other. Lift that one. Drag it forward. Put it down.

It was easier if he didn't think about it.

He took his eyes off the ruts and looked toward the fires. The moment he saw them he forgot all about his feet.

The lights of the fires had grown fainter.

Shana was just behind him. He could feel she had stopped too. He turned to look at her. His glance moved past her to the sky. Low down, over the land, a frail arc of brightness showed against the dark.

They had walked all night. Day was breaking.

Without anyone suggesting it, they dropped to the ground. They sprawled there watching the light grow stronger. The sun rose in the same sudden way it had set. They waited gratefully for its warmth to reach them.

It was Hester who looked back toward the west first.

"Gypsies." She struggled to her feet. "Gypsy caravans."

Henry managed to stand up too. A mile or two away, against the skyline, was a great jumble of carts and tents. Some of the carts did look like the caravans he had seen Gypsies driving in Ireland. They had the same high rounded roofs built over them.

Covered wagons, Henry thought. Real covered wagons.

It was like seeing Abraham Lincoln. Not a picture of him, or an actor in a film. But Lincoln himself.

"We'd better go on," Hester suggested. "It isn't far now."

It was all Henry could do to stand on his feet. He

wanted to lie down and sleep forever in the sun. But he knew Hester was right. Those wagons and tents looked as settled as a city. But he could see men and horses moving among them now. If the wagon train moved on while they were sleeping they might never get as close to it again.

Shana was the last to get up. Henry could see she had been crying. Her face was streaked with dust and tears. She looked at Henry as though she had never seen him before.

He felt suddenly shy with her. Now that she was two years older, she was no longer the easy natural friend he had known in the copper mine. She was a young woman and a stranger.

It was good to feel the sun on his back as he stumbled on. He guessed they had about two more miles to go. He tried to figure out how many steps that was. He started to count them.

He had reached a hundred several times. He had forgotten how many. There were men standing around him. Funny looking men in dark baggy clothes. Dark baggy trousers tucked into their boots like firemen. Square beards. They weren't offering him coffee or bacon sandwiches. They were staring at him with their hard blue eyes.

"We're looking for Kevin O'Neill," he heard Hester say. "Kevin O'Neill."

Some of the beards moved up and down. Others wagged from side to side.

"Nine. Nine. Nine," the men were saying. "Nine. Nine. Nine."

Henry couldn't stand upright any longer. He dropped to his knees. He lay down on the ground.

"O'Neill," Hester's voice said again.

This time the men's answer meant even less to him than "nine" had. Several of them broke out in a flow of barking and neighing. The sound went on over Henry's head.

It was worse than the night at Kevin's house.

At least the people he had found there spoke English.

Thirty-four

HENRY slept.

He was sweating when he woke up. His shirt was sticking to his back and the collar was hot and damp around his neck. His tongue felt enormous. It was like a piece of dead wood that had been pushed into his mouth. He kept wanting to spit it out. His lips were too dry to spit.

He sat up. The bearded men were gone. Shana and the Sullivans were lying on the ground a few feet away from him. He thought at first they were all asleep.

Shana wasn't. Her great dark eyes were open. She didn't smile when she saw Henry was awake. She didn't look as if it made any difference to her.

"Thada." He tried to say her name. He couldn't get his tongue out of the way to make the right sounds. Slowly, resting for a moment on his knees, he stood up. The nearest wagon was a hundred yards away.

It seemed to take a long time to reach it. One of the bearded men was squatting on the ground, doing something to a wheel.

"Water." Henry managed to get the word out.

The man was tugging at the wheel spokes.

"Water." It didn't seem to be Henry's own voice, but it was louder this time.

The man pulled the wheel off. He shook his head without turning around. Henry heard something that sounded like "Floose."

The man put the wheel on the ground. He jabbed his finger through the air in an angry way.

"Floose!" he repeated.

Without thinking what he was doing, Henry obeyed the jabbing finger. Tents, carts, horses, cattle, bearded men, camp fires, wagon after wagon. There seemed no end to them as he stumbled on.

Then at last he saw what "Floose" meant. Ahead of him was a broad clear river.

He didn't stop to take off any of his clothes. He waded in up to his knees. Splashing forward like a dog, he let the wonderful cool water cover him. He raised his face and drank from his cupped hands.

Even his feet stopped hurting. The thing in his mouth was his own tongue again. He splashed about for a few minutes longer. The thought of Shana began to worry him. He must find something to carry water in.

He climbed out and began to search along the bank. There was plenty of rubbish lying around. Great heaps of it everywhere. Rotting vegetables, bones, scraps of leather harness, broken wheels, splinters of pottery and china. Flies crawled all over it in the sun. There was a smell like an open drain. Henry forced himself to keep searching. There wasn't a single tin can anywhere. What did they do with them? Any other garbage dump in the world, he thought.

But maybe not in 1849, Henry remembered. Maybe they hadn't invented tin cans yet. They didn't seem to have invented empty bottles either. Or if they had, they didn't throw them away. At last he found a gray stone jug. The neck and handle were broken off, but it would still hold water. It smelled quite pleasantly of burnt sugar. He rinsed it carefully in the river before filling it.

The Sullivans were still asleep. Shana sat up as he stopped beside her. He handed her the jug and helped her lift it. As soon as she had swallowed a few mouthfuls she could hold the jug steady without Henry's help.

"Thank you." The shyness was still there between them, but she had lost some of that scared, watchful look.

Henry woke the others. They all had a drink of water. They sat there deciding how to try to find Kevin.

"It's a big camp," Henry explained. "It looked to me as if it went on for miles. All along this side of the river. If we start at one end and walk right through it . . ."

"We're sure to see him," Martin put in excitedly.

"Y-e-s." Henry didn't want to sound too hopeful. He still had that same uneasy feeling. Something had gone wrong. He hadn't thought quite the right words when he brought them here.

"At least we're bound to find someone who speaks English," he said. He could feel sure of that. Wherever they were, they were certainly in America. There must be some Americans around.

"We'll have a wash in the river first," Hester suggested. "And then we'll start."

"Ear lender?"

Henry jumped up at the sudden barking sound behind him. One of the bearded men was standing there. There was another man with him. He was a younger man, younger than Henry's father. He wore the same kind of boots and rough baggy clothes as all the other men Henry had seen in the camp. He had a mustache but no beard.

"He means, are you folks Irish?" The younger man stepped forward. " 'Ear lender,' that's the German for 'Irish.' "

"We are." Hester and Johnchristopher were smiling with relief at meeting someone who spoke English without even having to look for him. "We're from County Cork," Johnchristopher added. "Around Skibbereen."

"I wouldn't know about that." The younger man didn't smile. "I'm from back East myself." He made a gesture with his hand. The bearded German walked away. "I heard you got into camp this morning. I thought I'd come over and see how you're fixed." Henry could tell he was trying to sound friendly.

"We're the Sullivans." Hester didn't seem to notice how false his friendliness sounded. She and Johnchristopher stood up. "This is my husband, Johnchristopher. And I'm Hester."

Johnchristopher showed his white fan of teeth. He held out his hand. The man from back East shook it hurriedly.

"And this is our son, Martin." Martin jumped up, smiling too. The man only nodded to him. He was looking at Shana.

"I'm Shana O'Neill."

Henry always admired the proud way Shana said that. It was like someone saying she was the last of a great people. She didn't stand up.

The man took a long time turning his head away from her.

It was Henry's turn to introduce himself.

"Henry Travers," he said. "How do you do?"

"Well, what do you know." The man from back East smiled for the first time as he shook Henry's hand.

"What do you know," he repeated. "The same as me. My name's Henry Travers too."

Thirty-five

"THEN across the Atlantic on a coffin ship," Henry said.

Travers had taken them back to his wagon. They were sitting around his camp fire eating corn bread, dipping it into a pan of warm water to soften it. Henry was doing his best to answer Travers' questions about how they had got here.

"You came over from Ireland on a coffin ship, Henry?" Travers sounded suspicious.

"No, not me." Henry was glad he was sitting down. He had to do a lot of quick thinking to make his story convincing. He was glad the Sullivans were letting him do it alone. They might have tried to tell the truth, about thinking themselves here. He knew Travers would decide they were all crazy if they told him that.

"I joined up with the others in Missouri," he went on. "Pap took sick and died." He was trying to talk the way Tom Sawyer did. "And the Sullivans came by, heading west, so I trailed along with them."

"On foot?" Travers was looking at Shana. He still sounded suspicious.

"Land sakes, no." Tom Sawyer was always saying "land sakes," wasn't he? Or was it Aunt Polly? "The wagon broke down," he hurried on. "Then the Sullivans had to sell their horses. We joined another family for a ways, but they were fixing to settle a few miles back, so we came the rest of the way on foot."

"Traveling by night," Martin put in.

"Mostly by night." Henry frowned at Martin, trying to warn him to keep out of it. "It was too hot, days, and we ran out of water."

Travers seemed to believe him. He took his eyes off Shana, looking at each of them carefully in turn. At Johnchristopher's bandaged feet. At Martin's tight clothes. At Henry's own faded jeans.

Henry didn't like the way he did it. It made him feel as though they were things in a store and Travers was trying to figure out how much they were worth to him.

"So you're all pretty much destitute now," Travers said. "Pretty much dependent on other people's kindness."

"My brother Kevin'll take care of us." Shana stood up. "Thank you for the bread."

Henry stood beside her. He was glad Shana wanted to leave. He wanted to get away from Travers too. It wasn't only the fact that they had the same name. Henry realized that didn't have to mean anything. It didn't have to mean what he was afraid it might, anyway. Travers, even Henry Travers, wasn't such an unusual name.

The truth was Henry didn't like the man. He wouldn't have liked him whatever his name was. He didn't like the figuring way he looked at people. Especially not the way he looked at Shana.

He was looking at her now.

"Of course, Kevin'll take care of you," Travers said. "When you find him."

"Do you know Kevin?"

"Where is he?"

"Is he here?"

The Sullivans were all leaning forward.

"Yeah, I know him." Travers kept his eyes on Shana. "Kevin O'Neill. Tall fellow. Irish. About thirty years old. Good education. Sure, I know him." He was watching her to see if she believed him. "Has a way of smiling with one side of his mouth."

"Yes."

"It's a good while since I saw him last." Travers picked up the scraps of corn bread. "He came through here about a month ago. Traveling alone on horseback with a couple of pack mules."

"A month ago?" Shana pulled at her dress. She did it the way Henry's mother straightened her glasses when she was trying not to show how upset she was.

"Must have been at least a month." Travers wrapped the bread in a piece of cloth. "The way he was going, traveling light like that, he must be half-way to California by now."

Thirty-six

THEY had to accept Travers' offer. There wasn't any choice.

They had to get to California to find Kevin. Travers offered to take them there. All they had to do was work for him.

Johnchristopher would work as a teamster, taking care of the horses and cattle. Later, on the trail, he would drive one of Travers' three wagons. Hester would cook and wash clothes. Shana would help her. Martin and Henry would cut wood for the fires, fetch water, run errands, little chores like that.

They would none of them get paid for their work. They would be fed. They would have blankets and a dry place to sleep. They would be given the clothes and boots they needed. They would travel in Travers' wagons as soon as he was ready to start west.

It sounded all right.

Shana was against it from the first. She hated Travers. He didn't seem to notice it. He was nicer to her than he was to the others. The rough woolen clothes he found for Henry and Martin hung on them like sacks. He wouldn't let Hester shorten the sleeves and trousers either. They had to roll them up. The new dress he gave Shana fit her. So did the soft cowhide boots. If there was a piece of meat left in the stew after Travers had filled his own plate, Shana got it. He even let her sit down and rest sometimes during the day.

He couldn't stand to see any of the others doing nothing for a second. Johnchristopher and Travers' Indian teamster, Redfoot, drove the cattle across the river at dawn. They found grassland for them. They herded and guarded them all day while they grazed. They drove them back at sunset. They took turns keeping watch all night, so that none of the animals could stray or get stolen.

For over a hundred years Johnchristopher had slept whenever he felt like it. In the copper mine they had all made their own nights and days. They had probably slept sometimes for weeks at a time, Henry thought. After two days in the camp Redfoot had to keep an eye on Johnchristopher in case he dropped off in the saddle.

When Hester wasn't making bread or peeling potatoes or cutting up turnips or cooking, she was heating water and scrubbing and mending and hanging out washing every minute of daylight. There were few women in the camp. Some of the Germans had their families with them. Most of the men were traveling alone or with their partners. They were glad to bring their laundry and darning to Hester. Travers was glad to take their money for it.

Travers wasn't going to California to look for gold. He was taking his own gold with him, he said. His three wagons were piled with sacks of flour, sugar, coffee, tea, sides of bacon, barrels of whiskey, kettles and clothes and guns. He kept buying more from anyone who would sell to him. "Anything that's worth a dollar here," he told Henry, "will be worth ten dollars in California." Henry and Martin were on their feet all day, carrying and packing and loading and reloading Travers' wagons.

Henry didn't mind the work. All he minded was Travers. Travers was one of those people who can never watch you do anything without telling you a better way to do it.

There were other things bothering Henry too.

After a day or two he began to understand about the camp. It was a staging point. Wagon trains arrived there from all over the East. Axles and harnesses were mended, the oxen rested and grazed. Men met and talked about routes and gold and supplies and gold and guns. And gold. Little by little a group would form, twenty or thirty wagons, sixty or seventy men. They would elect a captain. Make a list of rules for the journey. Swear on a Bible to keep those rules. Then pull out across the river to the West. Although there were thousands of people in the camp, they were changing all the time. Few of them had been there more than a week or would stay more than another few days.

Travers had been there a month.

He still showed no sign of joining any of the groups. He was too busy buying up everything he could get his hands on. He talked about finding another wagon. It looked as though it was going to be another month at least before he thought about pulling out.

What worried Henry about that was that he knew something nobody else did.

Kevin wasn't going to reach California. He was going to be captured by Indians. Jane had told him that. Which Indians? Where? When?

The more time went by, the harder it was going to be to find Kevin.

Shana worried Henry even more than that. She was like a different person since she had come to America. He kept remembering what The Lieutenant had said. "She must have been a wild little girl." She hadn't seemed wild in the copper mine. But she did now. She kept looking at Travers the way she must have looked at that British officer. The one she had tried to shoot. The thought of her doing that to Travers scared Henry so much it kept him awake at night.

He tried to talk to Shana about it one morning. He told her that shooting a rich American could cause even more trouble than shooting British officers. She didn't seem to care. "We can always go back to the copper mine if they try to arrest me," Shana said. "Perhaps we can't think up anything we want here. But we can always go home. Just like we did that night from Kevin's house."

Henry could see it was no use arguing with her.

It wasn't that he would miss Travers. He didn't think he would feel too bad if Travers did get his head blown off. Except for one thing. That creepy business of their having the same name.

There was no way Henry could ever find out if that meant what he was afraid it did. Travers couldn't tell him. Travers didn't know his own future, if he would get married later and have a family. He didn't know what would become of that family if he did. He certainly didn't know if he would have a great-grandson who would teach in a college in the Hudson Valley. And call his son Henry.

But if Travers *did* happen to be Henry's great-great-grandfather, that was what was going to happen one day.

Unless something went wrong. Unless something got changed.

That was what kept Henry awake at night, thinking and worrying about that.

He knew he and Shana could change things "outside." They had changed The Lieutenant's memory of the night of Kevin's death by going to his house. Shana could change Travers' whole life now in an instant. With one of his own guns. She could end it.

What would happen to Henry if she did? If Shana shot his great-great-grandfather before he had any children? Would Henry never be born? Never exist?

But he did exist. He could feel himself lying under the wagon, wrapped in a blanket, wishing he could stop thinking about it and go to sleep.

Would he cease to exist then? Suddenly vanish.

Would Henry disappear, like the echo of a shot, without leaving even a memory behind him?

Thirty-seven

THE one thing that made Henry's life happier in the camp was being friends with Redfoot.

Redfoot was the first Indian Henry had ever known. He was a Ute. He didn't wear feathers or anything Henry thought of as Indian clothes. He wore the same kind of baggy trousers as most of the other men and a leather jacket without any sleeves. He had a round hard hat like Charlie Chaplin's but his long hair was straight. He smiled at Henry the first evening as they were eating their turnip stew. Nights, when he couldn't sleep, Henry would go and sit with him while he guarded the cattle.

Redfoot spoke English as well as Henry did. Sometimes he left out some of the smaller words like "the" and "is," as though he couldn't be bothered with them. When they were talking Henry started to leave them out too.

One night when Henry had been in camp a week they were sitting by the fire away from the wagons. The cattle were drowsing and munching around them. Redfoot could tell by the sound of their movements when any of them strayed. One of the things Henry liked about him was that often Redfoot was silent for long stretches of time. Henry could stare into the fire and feel his friend was there without having to say anything.

"Travers lied," Redfoot said suddenly.

Henry looked up to show he was listening. He didn't ask what Travers had lied about. Redfoot would tell him when he was ready.

"Your friend. Travers said it was month ago Kevin left."

"Kevin?" Henry couldn't keep silent any longer. "When did he leave?"

"Only two, three days before you came."

Henry figured quickly. That meant Kevin was ten days ahead of them, maybe two hundred miles. A week ago they might have caught up with him somehow. It was too late now. He could guess Travers had lied on purpose to keep them here.

"When you think Travers start west?" he asked.

"Better not wait. Find Kevin."

Henry agreed with that. He didn't think he was ever going to get a night's sleep until Shana was away from Travers.

"Kevin travel ten days already," he said. "We never catch him."

"You find. Easy."

"How?"

"Kevin with my people."

That startled Henry. Somehow he hadn't expected Kevin to be living with the Indians yet. "Your people capture him already?" he asked.

Redfoot smiled. "Not capture. I send Kevin to my people's camp on White River."

"Why?"

"He want go hunting, trapping furs in mountains. Utes help him."

The Lieutenant had got the story wrong, Henry

saw. Or perhaps it was Jane who had made up the part about Kevin being captured by Indians.

"How far is the White River?" he asked. He was too excited to leave out the small words.

"Two, three days."

"Walking?"

"Horse."

"We haven't got any horses."

"Travers buy two more today."

Henry felt in his shirt pocket. He had a five-dollar bill his father had sent him in Ireland. He looked at it in the firelight. There was another scrap of paper folded inside it. Henry recognized the announcement Kevin had put in the Skibbereen paper. It was strange to think it would be another fifty years before the newspaper printed it.

It was the same in a way with the five-dollar bill. It had Lincoln's picture on it. Lincoln wouldn't be president for about ten years yet. His face wasn't on any of the money they used now in the camp. He folded it around the announcement from the Skibbereen paper again and put it back in his pocket.

Redfoot watched him. He smiled. "We don't buy horses. Borrow them."

"Who from?"

"Travers."

Henry didn't think that would work. Travers wasn't the kind to lend anything to anyone. He said so.

"We don't ask," Redfoot explained.

Henry thought about that. He was sure Kevin would return the horses later.

"We'll need six horses," he said.

"Two."

"You and me and Shana and Johnchristopher . . ." Henry was counting on his fingers.

Redfoot shook his head. "Only you and me go."

Henry could see it would be easier to borrow two horses than six.

It would make less noise and they wouldn't be missed so much. At the same time he didn't want to leave Shana behind, to leave her for even another day with Travers.

"Shana's Kevin's sister," he told Redfoot. "We take Shana. Three horses."

"Two."

Redfoot had made up his mind. He wouldn't take anyone but Henry to the camp on the White River. He wouldn't say why until Henry asked him right out.

"We pass wagon train. See Indian with white girl."

There was something about the way he said it that made Henry stop arguing at once.

"When we go?" he asked.

Redfoot stood up and threw some sticks on the fire. He was smiling. He was enjoying his own silence, as though he had a surprise for Henry and it was fun thinking about it as long as he could without telling him what it was.

"We go now," Redfoot said.

Thirty-eight

REDFOOT had everything planned. He had everything ready.

Not far away, by the river, were two horses. There were saddles on them. Their reins were tied to pegs in the ground. Across their backs behind the saddles were supplies for the journey, roped up in blanket rolls.

Henry had only been on a horse twice before in his life. Both times at a holiday camp in the Catskills where he had spent a month one summer. He knew what riding felt like, how far away the ground seemed when you were sitting in a saddle. He knew how to hold the reins and put his feet in the stirrups. That was all he knew.

Redfoot gave him a leg up and helped him onto the smaller horse. Henry sat there, holding the pommel. Redfoot untied the reins and led both horses away from the camp. After a few minutes they reached a place where there was a bar across the river. Redfoot jumped onto his own horse in a single movement. He kept hold of both sets of reins and headed away from the bank.

The water rose slowly. It covered Henry's feet. It crept up to his knees. There was a horrible minute when the animal under him scrambled about trying to stay on its hooves. Henry's feet began to feel cold. They had only felt wet before. He realized his boots were clear of the water. The horse lurched and bounded up the bank. The pommel hit Henry in the chest. He managed to cling to it. Redfoot handed him the reins. They started west across the dark plain.

They rode on all night. Soon after dawn they reached a small stream and stopped to eat and water the horses. When Henry climbed down from his saddle the ground felt so still and so solid under his feet it took him a moment to get used to standing on it.

They rested for a few minutes and ate some corn bread while the horses rounded their long necks and chewed at the grass.

When they rode on they were still following the western trail. Hundreds of wagons, thousands of horses and oxen had left a worn strip across the plain. Every few miles were burnt patches of grass and scatterings of smelly litter where one of the parties had camped for the night. The shape of mountains appeared out of the haze ahead. Redfoot turned left away from the trail. Henry's horse followed him. The ground sloped upward. There was more grass, more trees. Redfoot stopped from time to time. They let the horses graze without getting down from their saddles.

There were no houses, no fences, no paths. Only the land. It was as though no one had ever been there before them. At first Henry was struck by the silence. There seemed to be no sound but the soft beat of hooves, the creaking of the saddles. But, listening, he could hear that the stillness itself was made up of dozens of tiny sounds. The movement of leaves and blades of grass, the call of birds, humming insects, the rustle of a distant stream, the quick passage of other living things around him. For an hour or two Henry felt he could see and hear everything more clearly than he ever had in his life.

That feeling was gone long before noon. By the time the sun was halfway up the sky Henry's world had shrunk to a very few, close things. No matter how he shifted in the saddle the strap of his left stirrup cut into his leg just above the knee. There was an endless ache in the small of his back. All his eyes saw was a pommel, the black jogging mane of his horse, its ears flickering when a fly settled on them. Everything else had ceased to be there.

They rested for a few hours that night by the side of a mountain stream. Redfoot didn't light a fire. They ate some more corn bread and a mush of cold beans. They rolled up in their blankets and slept. Before it was daylight they rode on again.

If you travel for long enough without arriving, you begin to feel you have never done anything else. The second and third days were just like the first for Henry. For an hour or two in the morning everything was marvelously clear. The country altered slowly around him. Rocks changed to grass slopes and trees and then back to rocks as they crossed another spur of the mountains. By noon it had all narrowed down to the few things closest to his eyes and the aching of his own body.

It was the afternoon of the third day when they came to the White River. It was cooler here than it had been in the wagon camp. The country looked soft with a blue green color that made Henry think of the copper mine. He saw a straggle of smoke against the sky.

"My home." Redfoot turned in the saddle and called to him.

Soon Henry could see the great tall tents in the bend of the river. Redfoot stopped his horse. Without a sound that Henry could hear a man appeared out of the trees ahead of him. He looked more like Henry's idea of an Indian than Redfoot. His hair was braided and hung in two plaits over his bare chest. There were several necklaces of long white pointed teeth around his neck. His leather trousers were much tighter than Redfoot's, except around his ankles where they widened out like a sailor's. His feet were wrapped in some kind of skins laced together with thongs.

Redfoot jumped down and ran to meet him. They stood with their arms around each other in silence. Redfoot said something Henry couldn't understand. The other answered. Redfoot leapt back on his horse in his usual way without using the stirrups. His friend leapfrogged up behind him.

"Kevin in his lodge," Redfoot called back to Henry. "I show you."

Kevin's lodge was a big round tent made of skins. It was set a little apart from the others. Redfoot rode on. Henry pulled back the tent flap and stepped inside. There was a smell of wood smoke and coffee and an animal warmth that made him think of the bear house in the zoo.

Something moved. Henry saw the stir of a white hand in the dusk.

"Kevin?" he asked softly.

A man got up from a heap of furs. He was tall with black hair and dark eyes. He looked enough like the picture in the Sullivans' cottage for Henry to recognize him at once.

A lot of different thoughts were tangled up in

Henry's mind as he looked at him. This was the end of his journey. The end of his search. But it wasn't the first time they had met. The last time he had seen Kevin, he had been an old man, dying.

The clearest thought, though, the one that surprised him, was that Kevin didn't look as much like Shana as he had expected.

He reminded Henry much more of Jane.

Thirty-nine

"SHANA'S here? In America?"

Kevin was shouting with excitement. He couldn't keep still. He kept pacing up and down inside the tent. He clapped his hands together. He waved them about.

"Where?" he asked. "Where? Where is she?"

Henry sat down. He told Kevin where Shana was. He told him about the Sullivans and about working for Travers.

Kevin looked happier at every word he said. He frowned when Henry got to Travers, then he smiled again. He smiled with one side of his mouth. Henry liked the way he did it, as though Kevin was making fun of himself.

"How did they get there?" he asked Henry. "Were they on that coffin ship with me? How did we get separated? Was it when I had that fever? Did they think I was dead?"

Henry was glad he was asking so many questions at once. It made it easier not to answer any of them. He knew from what The Lieutenant had told him that Kevin didn't remember anything about the copper mine. He didn't want to have to explain to him about that. Most of all he didn't want to have to explain how they had all thought themselves here across five thousand miles and back over a hundred years in time. It would take too long and he was very tired.

"You'd better ask Shana how she got to America," he said. "She was looking for you in the wagon camp and Redfoot told me you were here so we rode over together."

"I know." Kevin used the word the way Mrs. Regan did. He meant he understood.

He lifted the furs and started pulling out things. A pan. A spoon and knife. A sack of flour. A book. He put them all on a blanket. The quick way he did it made Henry think of Jane collecting the picnic that day on Horse Island. It gave him a shock to remember how far away in the future that day was.

"How long did it take you to get here?" Kevin was roping up a bedroll with all the things inside it.

"Three days," Henry told him. "We hardly slept at all."

"We can make it in less time than that if we take an extra horse." Kevin finished knotting the rope. He stood up. "Let's go."

"Now?"

Henry's voice didn't seem to come out of his own mouth. It was as though someone else had spoken the word. He could hear the horror in it. He could understand it too. The idea of climbing back into that saddle was enough to make anyone cry out like that.

Kevin was standing looking down at him. There was something about him Henry had noticed at once. Even when Kevin was quite still, he seemed to be moving. He was like a generating plant Henry had once visited with his father. You couldn't see any wheels turning but you could feel the force inside.

"You want to stay here and rest?" Kevin's eyes were kind.

Henry nodded gratefully. "Yes, please."

"I'll ask Redfoot to take you back to the camp in a couple of days."

"No." Henry never wanted to see that saddle again. Not even in a couple of days. "I'll wait for you here," he said firmly.

"Wait?" Kevin turned in the entrance of the tent. "I'm not coming back."

"Not coming back?" Henry made a great effort to bring his tired mind to understand that. "Where are you going?"

"Back East." Kevin squatted on his heels in front of him.

"This is no place for Shana," he went on. "She'll have to go to school. I'll take her and the Sullivans and we'll go to Philadelphia. I'll settle there. Start a business. Making furniture. I've done a lot of carpentry. Then branch out into building. I'll go into politics later . . ."

Kevin was talking more to himself than to Henry. Five minutes ago he had been all set to go trapping in the mountains with his Indian friends. Now he was planning a completely different future for himself. He probably didn't have a cent in his pocket, but he was thinking of becoming Governor of Pennsylvania. Henry knew he could do it, too. He was the kind of man who never thought about the difficulties of anything. Unlike Shana and the Sullivans Kevin hadn't lost the gift of getting anything he wanted when he left the copper mine. There was nothing magic about it. He would just make things happen his way.

He was standing up again. "I'll never forget what you've done for me," he said. "Coming here to tell me about Shana. If you're ever in Philadelphia look me up. You can count on me."

He had his bedroll over his shoulder. He was moving toward the entrance to the tent.

"No!" That other person inside Henry's tired body, the one who was doing all the thinking for him, had cried out in horror again.

Kevin was holding aside the tent flap.

"I can't stay here alone," Henry heard his own voice say. "You'll be gone by the time I get back to that camp with Redfoot. So will Shana and the Sullivans. And I'll never . . . never . . ."

Henry couldn't say it, but he knew what he meant. He would never be able to get back into his own time. He would be stuck here alone, over a hundred years ago, forever. He would never see any of the people in his own life again.

He would be dead long before his mother and father were even thought of.

Forty

HENRY had felt lonely many times in his life. But never as lonely as he felt at that moment.

The terrible thing was that he couldn't explain any of it to Kevin. He didn't know how to start to tell him the truth. He had to find some other way of saying it.

"Shana and the Sullivans are like . . . they're like my family too," he said slowly. "They're the only family I've got. Here. Now. I don't mind staying so much if I can stay with them and we all get older at the same time together. But I can't . . . I just can't do it without them."

"Right." Kevin dropped the tent flap. He was a man who had no trouble making quick decisions. "You get some sleep then. We'll start out in the morning and ride back together."

He picked up one of the fur robes and wrapped it around Henry. It was the last thing Henry felt before he dropped into the darkness of sleep.

It was still dark when Henry woke up. Perhaps he had been dreaming about Jane, because for a moment he thought he was in that empty house on the island with her. He felt the thick, slightly sticky fur of the robe Kevin had spread over him. He remembered everything.

He tried not to worry about it. It wouldn't be so

bad. They would all go to Philadelphia together. He guessed he would go to school there. It was going to be strange going to school all this long ago, because he knew a lot of things none of the other boys would. He knew about electricity and cars and airplanes. None of those things had been invented yet.

Maybe when he grew up he could invent some of them himself. The idea made him smile. It didn't make him smile for long. He saw all the trouble that could lead to. What would the Wright Brothers do if Henry came along and invented an airplane before they did? They might have to go on fixing bicycles all their lives. And what about Lindbergh? If Henry invented an airplane now, say within the next ten years, someone was likely to fly the Atlantic alone long before Lindbergh. The North and South might even use Henry's invention in the Civil War. It was terrifying to think what that could lead to. Thousands of people being bombed to death who would have gone on living except for Henry. He could see why the Sullivans were always talking about "not changing things outside."

He wouldn't invent anything, Henry decided. Ever.

He was far too wide-awake to go back to sleep now. There was a faint light where the flap of the tent wasn't closed. Henry crawled toward it.

It looked like midnight in the Indian camp. There was no one to be seen. A fire was still smouldering a few yards away. He found some sticks and kindled it back into flames. The sky was bright with a great wash of stars. He lay beside the fire and looked up at them.

Even if he kept clear of inventing things, he realized, he would still have to be careful how he lived. Anything he did might change someone's life. He could see that was always true of everyone in the world. If you won a prize, another boy didn't. But it was true of Henry in a special way now. He was different from everybody else. He wasn't supposed to be here. He wasn't supposed to have been born yet.

He could imagine how strange he would seem to other people if they found that out.

He thought about school in Philadelphia again. He would have to watch out every second not to give himself away. Maybe he'd get used to it after a while, but at first he would have to keep reminding himself it was 1849.

"Eighteen forty-nine," Henry said aloud. "It's eighteen forty-nine."

He wondered who the President of the United States was.

History was going to be a dangerous subject. He could see that. It wasn't only what he didn't know. Who was alive and who wasn't. Was Benjamin Franklin still living in 1849? Thomas Jefferson? There were all the things he did know too. He was probably the only person in the world at that moment who knew Abraham Lincoln was going to be assassinated in about fifteen years' time.

It was frightening to realize this.

It was all the more frightening because he might also be the only person in the world who could stop it. He could write to Lincoln and tell him about John Wilkes Booth, warn him not to go to the theater.

"Never change things outside."

But, still, to have the chance to save Lincoln's life. And not do anything about it.

The world would be a lot happier place if Lincoln had lived a few years longer. Henry's history teacher had often said that.

There was something about Lincoln, more than anyone else, that made Henry feel serious. Almost solemn. He reached into his shirt pocket and pulled out the five-dollar bill. He wanted to look at Lincoln's face while he thought it all out.

The money was folded into a neat square, just as he had put it there. It wasn't until he had straightened it out that he saw something was wrong. Something was missing.

The piece of newspaper with Kevin's announcement wasn't folded inside the five-dollar bill.

Henry knew he hadn't lost it. It hadn't blown away on the journey.

He knew exactly what had happened to it.

It had ceased to exist.

It had ceased to exist because things had changed now. Kevin knew where Shana was. He wasn't going to spend the rest of his life looking for her. He would never put that announcement in the paper.

Henry couldn't think about anything for a moment. It was as though someone had hit him on the forehead with a hammer. He felt stunned and dizzy and slightly sick.

Thoughts soon began to gallop through his head again. Awful, headlong thoughts. Black as Ulalus.

Henry had changed Kevin's whole future now. Kevin wasn't going to stay with the Utes and go trapping. He was going back East to Philadelphia. He wasn't going to live the same life at all. He wasn't going to marry the same girl, or have the same daughter, or go back to Ireland to look for Shana, or buy the same house there, or have the same grandson, The Lieutenant, or . . . All that was going to cease to exist like that piece of paper.

None of it was going to happen.

Jane was never going to be born.

Forty-one

HENRY left the tent flap open behind him. He could just see the pile of furs where Kevin slept. He walked over to it. He had made up his mind what he was going to do.

He wasn't choosing between Shana and Jane, he told himself. It was more like choosing between the copper mine and the islands. Jane was like him. She lived outside where days came and went without anyone being able to stop them. She couldn't learn math or get dressed in the morning or sail to the islands just by thinking she'd done it. She went to awful boarding schools. She had trouble with her parents. She had a right to be born and work it all out for herself. He wasn't going to interfere with that.

Kneeling down, Henry felt for Kevin's shoulder to shake him awake. His fingers gripped into the fur. There was nobody there.

Henry had spent a whole hour deciding exactly what to say. Suddenly there was no one to say it to. It made him feel hopeless for a moment.

It wasn't so bad, when he thought about it. He was sure Kevin hadn't left without him. He had said they would start in the morning together. He wasn't the kind to break a promise. All he had to do was wait until Kevin got back. He thought he'd better keep awake while he waited.

There was a wooden box beside the pile of furs. Henry found a candle on it. He took it outside to light it from the fire.

Redfoot was sitting there, staring into the flames.

"You look for Kevin?" he asked.

"Where is he?"

"He went to see his friend. Ute girl. Other camp down the river. Kevin say good-bye to her."

It had all started. The things Henry had been afraid of. Kevin would have married that girl if he hadn't come here and told him about Shana.

"We leave now." Henry could make quick decisions too. "We start back to wagon camp right away."

"We wait for Kevin."

"No." It would be better if he never saw Kevin again.

"Why not?"

Henry wanted to tell him. He had a feeling Redfoot would believe him. He would understand about the mushrooms and the copper mine and Shana being over a hundred years old. He would understand about Jane having her own right to be born.

"Bad things happen if Kevin come back to wagon camp with us." There wasn't time to say more than that now. "Bad things for many people. For my friends."

"How you know?"

Henry lifted his hands and covered his eyes. "In my head," he explained.

"You dream?"

"In a way."

Redfoot looked at him for a long time in silence. He turned away. "I saddle horses," he said.

Henry found the book in Kevin's bedroll. It was

called *Common Sense.* There was a pencil stuck in the back of the binder. Kevin had been marking some of the sentences in the book. Henry found a blank page at the end. He tore it out.

Using the wooden box as a table, Henry wrote what he had made up his mind to tell Kevin.

I LIED TO YOU. YOUR SISTER ISN'T AT THE
CAMP. IT WAS TRAVERS' IDEA. HE KNEW YOU
WERE LOOKING FOR SHANA AND YOUR FRIENDS.
HE SAID IF I BROUGHT YOU BACK HE COULD
TELL YOU THEY HAD GONE SOMEWHERE ELSE AND
MAKE YOU PAY TO FIND OUT WHERE. IT IS
ALL A LIE. SHANA WAS NEVER THERE AT ALL.
NEVER. TRAVERS HAS NEVER SEEN HER. SO
DON'T COME THERE. STAY HERE WITH THE
INDIANS. I KNOW YOU WILL HAVE A FINE LIFE
IF YOU DO.   HENRY.

Forty-two

IT was easier going back. Henry's body had got used to riding. His back didn't ache any more. Even the strap of the left stirrup hardly hurt his leg.

Redfoot left him twenty miles from the wagon camp. He wasn't going any farther. He didn't want to work for Travers again. He was going back to his own people on the White River.

They had talked a lot the night before.

Henry told Redfoot about his letter to Kevin. He told him the whole story to explain why he wrote it. Redfoot listened to it all in silence.

"You do what your heart tells you," he said when Henry had finished. He promised he would talk to Kevin himself when he got back to the White River.

"I tell him all Travers' lie," he said now as they parted. "I tell him forget Shana. Shana never in wagon camp."

Henry thanked him. He leant forward in his saddle. They put their hands on each other's shoulders. Redfoot turned his horse and cantered away. Henry rode on alone.

He was still in the high wooded country. A few more miles and he would reach the plain and the wagon trail.

He knew he would never see Redfoot again. He wished he knew what had happened to the Ute Indians, if they had been allowed to go on living in their own lands, leading their own lives. He would try to find a book about it when he got home, Henry thought.

It was at that moment, as he was thinking of home, that his horse reared up under him. He didn't grab at the pommel. He kept his feet in the stirrups and straightened in the saddle. The horse settled back onto its front legs. It stood quite still, its ears raised, listening.

Henry listened too. He thought at first it was the cry of a bird. It was thin and faint with two notes to it.

Someone was calling his own name.

Henry touched his reins against the neck of the horse. It moved forward. A shower of stones slithered down the bank on his left. A wildly running figure followed the stones. It came to a stop at the bottom of the slope.

"Henry."

Shana hurried toward him.

He jumped down and ran to her. She put her arms around him. "Thank God, Henry," she said. "Thank God, we've found you."

When Shana let go of him Henry could see first Martin, then Hester and Johnchristopher running down the same slope. They were as excited to see him as Shana was.

It made Henry feel awful. He had been thinking about them most of the last two days since he left the Indian camp. No matter how much he thought, he hadn't changed his mind. He had gone over it again all day yesterday. He would find them in the wagon camp and get them away by themselves. Then he'd lie to them. He'd tell them he hadn't found Kevin. He'd make them see it was hopeless to search for him any further.

But it's one thing to think about lying to your friends. It's another thing to do it. It's even more difficult when they're smiling at you and shaking your hand and saying, Thank God, they've found you.

"We didn't want to leave without you," Johnchristopher explained.

"But we had to."

"We couldn't stay any longer."

"One of the men in the camp . . ."

They were all helping each other along in their usual way.

". . . said you must have gone off with Redfoot."

"But we didn't know where."

"You didn't know where?" Of course they didn't, Henry remembered. He hadn't told anyone where he was going. Redfoot had the horses all saddled. They had ridden off at once.

"Travers was going to beat you when you got back," Shana told him.

"Because of the horses."

"We thought we'd look for you."

"As long as we could."

"As long as our food lasted," Hester explained.

"We came up in the hills in case there was anyone chasing us."

"After what happened."

"We had to go on the run," Martin put in excitedly.

"On the run?" Henry thought it was just Martin's way of talking. "Why?" he asked.

"Because I shot Travers."

Henry sat down.

"Shana?" he asked slowly. "You . . . Shot . . . Travers?"

Shana looked back at him steadily with her great dark eyes.

"I shot him dead," she said proudly.

Forty-three

HENRY looked down at himself.

He sat and stared at his own body. His feet were there. His knees, his legs, his chest, his shoulders and arms and hands. He couldn't see any more of himself than that. But he could hear with his ears and smell with his nose and taste with his tongue.

He hadn't ceased to exist.

Henry started to laugh.

They asked him what the matter was. They gathered around him, laughing too. They asked him what he was laughing at.

"It was just chance," Henry explained, trying to get his breath back. "Bad luck. Henry Travers. Having the same name as mine. He isn't my great-great-grandfather. He wasn't. He couldn't have been. Because I'm still here."

"We're all here now." Hester nodded. "So we might as well leave."

"If you'd like to, Henry?" Johnchristopher asked.

"Leave?" Henry looked around for the horse. It was grazing a few yards away. "Where do you want to go?"

"Home."

"We had a talk about it," Hester said. "And we decided this wasn't a good place for us."

"Even before I shot Travers," Shana agreed.

"There's something strange about it," Hester went on. "Children grow up too fast here." She looked at Shana. "We were all happier where we were."

"We've got to think about Kevin too," Shana told Henry. "How do we know he went to California? That's only what Travers said. We might go all the way out there and find he wasn't there. And in the meantime . . ."

"In the meantime Kevin may come back."

"He'll be coming any day now."

"Looking for us."

"In the copper mine."

"So we'd all like to go home," Hester finished.

It was exactly what Henry had hoped they would like. He wanted to go home too. It was all too much for him here, having to worry all the time that anything he did might spoil somebody else's life.

It wasn't only that, though, that made him want to go home. It was the thought of never seeing his parents again, either of them, anywhere.

"I miss the cottage," Hester was saying.

"And the long quiet evenings," Johnchristopher remembered. "And the long nights too."

"I miss the food," Martin said. "Fruit cake and lamb stew whenever I want it."

"I even miss the Ulalus."

Henry had been smiling until Shana said that. He had forgotten about the Ulalus. He had forgotten about Fowler. Now he remembered why he had been in such a hurry to leave the copper mine. He had no clear idea what would happen if people started looking for Fowler, if they traced him down the chimney, if they found his crushed bones in that cave. He had no more than a series of unpleasant pictures in his mind. Policemen and judges and bullying faces.

"Ready?" Hester asked.

Henry felt Shana take his hand on one side. Martin was already holding his other one.

If the police went down the mine looking for Fowler, Henry thought suddenly, they'd find Shana and the Sullivans. They'd question them. They'd bring them up into the daylight, into the present, the way Fowler would have done . . .

Hester and Johnchristopher and Shana and Martin had already closed their eyes.

Henry wanted to shout at them.

Stop.

Then he remembered that *he* was the one who had brought them to America. He was the one who had thought the words for all of them.

Did he still have that gift?

"We're all back where we were," Henry thought quickly. "We're all back there that afternoon before Fowler got killed."

Henry closed his eyes.

Forty-four

HENRY put out his hand and felt cautiously around. He was afraid to look. His fingers touched something soft and smooth. He grasped it and pinched it. He was no longer frightened. He knew what it was.

He opened his eyes. He was right. It was his pillow.

Through the window in front of him he could see the tall chimney of the copper mine. He was sitting on his own bed in his own room in Penelope's house.

He was wearing his own clothes, his own jeans and sneakers. There was no mud on them. He felt in his shirt pocket. He pulled out the five-dollar bill and unfolded it. Inside was the torn piece of newspaper.

"ANNOUNCEMENT," it said, and below that the names: "SHANA O'NEILL. JOHNCHRISTOPHER SULLIVAN . . . WILL ANYONE KNOWING THE PRESENT WHEREABOUTS . . ."

It was all right. He hadn't changed anything after all. Kevin had come back to Ireland still looking for Shana.

Jane had taken Henry to the island where he had found this announcement. So that was all right too.

Jane had been born.

"Where is she?" Someone was talking in the living room.

"She's after going to her work." That was Mrs. Regan's voice.

Henry hurried to the door and unlocked it. He paused at the top of the stairs.

"When do you expect her back?" He recognized the other voice too. He remembered the way it had yelled "Hey, kid" after him.

"Only herself could tell you that."

"What?"

The voices grew fainter. They were only sounds now. Angry, demanding American sounds. Then calm, patient Irish ones. Henry crept down three more stairs.

"For Pete's sake." It was a cry of anguish. Henry peered between the banisters.

Fowler was bending over the wastepaper basket beside the kitchen door.

"She never even opened them." He was holding several letters. Henry recognized the envelopes from the Bonoco Co., Inc., Urgent.

Mrs. Regan said something calm from the kitchen.

"What?" Fowler followed her inside.

Penelope's studio was only twenty yards from the house. Henry didn't knock at the door. He pushed it open and ran in. Penelope was sitting on a stool staring at a huge block of stone on the floor in front of her. She didn't look around as Henry closed the door behind him.

"Penelope." Henry could see it was going to be hard to get in touch with her. He raised his voice. "Penelope!"

She still didn't turn. He thought she nodded her head.

"There's a man here called Fowler," Henry hurried on. "He's from a mining company and you've got to talk to him. He'll get killed if you don't. I can't tell you how I know that. But I know he'll get killed!"

Penelope nodded again. "It's all wrong," she said softly. She was still staring at the block of stone. "I haven't even begun to get it right yet."

Henry remembered the first time he had seen her at the airport. He had known then she wasn't going to be easy to talk to. For once he was going to *make* her listen to him.

He looked on Penelope's work table until he found a hammer and chisel. He walked over to the block of stone. Bits of it had been hacked away here and there. Sticking up from one end was a thin curving stem. It looked like an unfinished arm reaching up toward the ceiling. Henry put the blade of the chisel against the bottom of it. He lifted the hammer.

"No!" Penelope was standing up. "Henry," she said. She had recognized him.

"I'll stop if you'll listen to me." Henry kept the hammer hovering in the air. "If you don't listen I'm going to hack this arm off."

"How did you know it was an arm?"

"I'm going to hack it off."

"All right." Penelope sat down on the stool again. "I'll listen. What is it?"

Henry decided she meant it. For the first time since he had known her she was looking straight into his eyes. "There's a man here called Fowler," he said. "He's from a mining company. He wants . . . He wants to tear open the copper mine . . ." There was something about Penelope's eyes that reminded him of Redfoot. They had the same openness, as though nothing they saw, nothing anyone said could surprise or change them.

Before he knew what he was doing Henry was telling her everything, about Shana and the Sullivans hiding in the mine during the famine and never growing any older . . .

Penelope didn't interrupt him. There was a long silence when Henry had finished. Penelope walked over to the window of her studio. She looked at the chimney at the top of the hill.

"All right," she said at last. "I'll talk to that man, Fowler. I own that whole hill. I own those cottages. And I own that chimney. I promise you, no one's going down that mine. If you ever see Fowler or anyone like him hanging around up there again, I'll have him arrested for trespassing."

She started to the door. Halfway there she stopped. She looked at the chimney again.

"Those idiots in the village," Penelope said. "I always knew they weren't ghosts living in that mine. Ghosts don't make smoke."

Forty-five

"I CAME to say good-bye."

Henry was sitting at the table in the Sullivans' cottage. It was the day after his talk with Penelope.

"I've got to go back to America," he explained.

"Back where we were?"

Henry could tell from Shana's voice that she didn't envy him. Hester and Johnchristopher looked sorry for him too. He could see they didn't any of them want to go back to America. Ever.

Their journey to the West hadn't been altogether useless though, Henry saw. Hester had some new pans hanging near the fire. They were the kind she used in the wagon camp. Johnchristopher had on a leather jacket without sleeves like Redfoot's. Shana was wearing a new pair of cowhide boots. Outside, Martin was riding a pony around the field. He was riding a Western saddle and twirling a lasso. They wouldn't have been able to think up any of those things for themselves if they hadn't seen them in America.

Hester brought him a piece of fresh corn bread and some milk. Johnchristopher asked him how long it would take to cross the Atlantic on a ship. Henry said he guessed it would take a long time.

The Sullivans said good-bye to him outside the cottage. They made Henry promise to come and see them the next time he was in Ireland. Shana led him up the twisting steps in the cliff. They passed the cave where the Ulalus lived. They stood together in the ring of candles for the last time.

"Thank you for trying to help us, Henry."

Shana held out her hand. Henry took it. Her fingers felt strong and lively in his.

"Will you promise me something, Shana?"

"What?"

"You won't try to leave the mine until Kevin comes back."

"All right."

"Promise."

"I promise."

Henry reached the top of the ladder. Shana was still standing in the ring of candles. She lifted her arm and waved to him when he looked back.

For the rest of the summer Henry went swimming in the cove. He bicycled over to The Lieutenant's house. He went sailing with Jane. They explored all the islands together, even the farthest ones.

When Henry flew back to America in September, his mother and father were both at the airport to meet him. They were living together at home again. His mother still went to New York a lot. She had a part-time job there helping to write a magazine. When Henry came home from school and found her making the beds she didn't seem so angry about it any more. She and Henry's father talked less like two strangers.

His father said Henry had changed too. He said he was less dreamy. He said Henry seemed to have learned to think for himself in Ireland.

Henry never told him how. It was easy being back in school. It was restful doing the same things every day. It was a relief not having to make decisions all the time.

He wrote to Jane at her boarding school almost every week. She wrote back funny letters about her mother's new husband. His name was Ronald.

Little by little as the color of the leaves changed and the first snows came to the Hudson Valley, Ireland began to seem farther and farther away.

But he never forgot Shana and the Sullivans. All kinds of things kept reminding him of them. The guard at the school gym. The smell of cypress trees. Lincoln's face on a coin.

He wondered if they were still safe in the copper mine. Still leading their happy, timeless lives, thinking their own nights and days, their own danger and safety, tiredness and rest.

Their own hopes.

Henry thought they were.

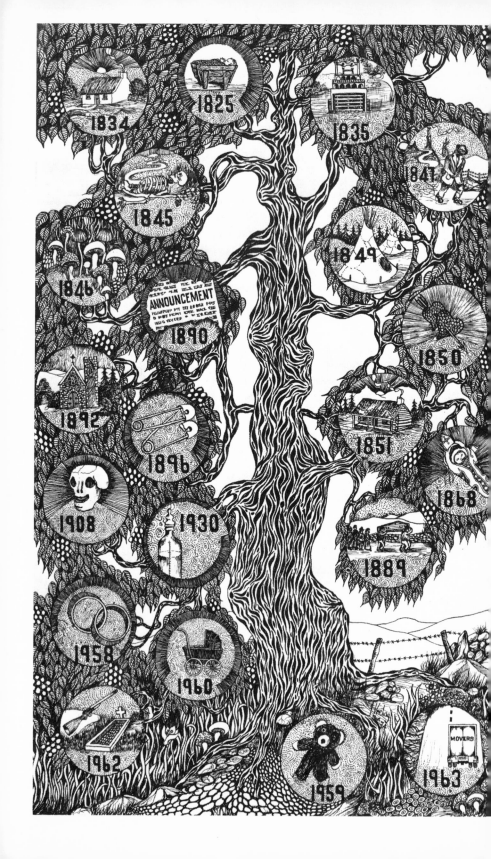

When it all happened

1825 Kevin O'Neill is born.
1834 Shana O'Neill is born.
1835 Mark Twain, author of *Tom Sawyer*, is born in Missouri.
1845 Beginning of the famine in Ireland.
1846 Kevin steals a sheep. He rescues the Sullivans from the soldiers. They all hide in the copper mine.
1847 Kevin leaves the mine. He sails to America. He comes back to life in a fever camp near Quebec.
1849 Kevin goes West. He lives with the Ute Indians.
1850 Kevin marries a Ute Indian girl.
1851 Kevin settles in Colorado.
1868 Kevin's daughter, Marguerite, is born.
1889 Kevin's wife dies.
1890 Kevin returns to Ireland with his daughter. He starts to run an announcement in the Skibbereen paper every week, searching for Shana and the Sullivans.
1892 Kevin's daughter, Marguerite, marries Michael Claire in Ireland.
1896 Kevin's grandson, Shaun Claire, "The Lieutenant," is born.
1908 Kevin dies.
1930 The Lieutenant's son, Dermot Claire, is born.
1958 Dermot Claire becomes Henrietta Wainwright's first husband.
1959 Henry Travers is born in South Dakota.
1960 Jane Claire is born in Ireland.
1962 Dermot Claire has an accident with a shotgun. Jane's mother, Henrietta, marries again for the first, but not the last time.
1963 Henry Travers moves to the Hudson Valley with his parents.

About the author

MARC BRANDEL was born in London, brought up mostly in Europe, and has spent much of his life in the United States. Now he lives with his wife and two daughters in the town of Ballydehob, County Cork, Ireland. His occupation is, and always has been, writing. He is the author of six novels, and his TV plays have been produced by every network in the United States and England, as well as in France, Germany, Holland, Sweden, Greece, and Yugoslavia.

F
BRA   Brandel, Marc

           The mine of lost
           days

DATE DUE

F
BRA   Brandel, Marc

           The mine of lost
           days

DISCARD

C.1

C.1

DATE DUE	BORROWER'S NAME	
APR 8	Christina K	210
	Randy P	212
FEB 14 '80	Lisa Davis	602
	Kat	